CONTENTS

MATEO'S LAW

ALL THINGS WESTERN

By S. Cox
ThunderTree

By Sandra Cox

**Western Romance and Western
Time Travel Romance**
TumbleStar
Montana Shootists
Sundial
Silverhills

AND MORE

Romantic Suspense with a touch of Paranormal
The Crystal
Amulets
Boji Stones
Rose Quartz
Black Opal

Paranormal Romance
Tall, Dark and Undead

Romantic Suspense
Queen of Diamonds

Regency Romance
Miss Redmond's Deception

Young Adult Series
Mutants
Love, Lattes, and Mutants
Love, Lattes, and Danger
Love, Lattes, and Angel
Hunter
Vampire Island
Moon Watchers
Vampire Bay
Cats of Catarau
Shardai
Akasha

Makita

Young Adult
Minder
Ghost For Sale

Anthologies
Parallels: Felix Was Here

Nonfiction
Flower Gardens and More
Power Stones

Retired
Odin Cats
Sunset

ALL RIGHTS RESERVED

A TIP OF THE HAT TO

Beta readers
Elizabeth Seckman
and
Chris Yockey
I couldn't have done it without you.

DEDICATED TO

Friend and author D. L. Finn

CHAPTER 1

A chill March wind lifted Chief Deputy Blair Delaney's ponytail and nipped her skin as she stepped out of the patrol car, snapping a twig beneath a sturdy boot. With a flick of her thumbs, she turned up her collar and burrowed deeper into her worn, brown bomber jacket.

The setting sun hovered on the horizon and outlined a dark-barked, bare-leaved oak that arced over the porch of Sheriff Mateo Grey's cabin.

The temperature dropped. A wolf howled.

She spun on her heel. The large gray predator stood at the edge of the property, watching her. As seconds ticked, he held her gaze but came no closer. Finally, as if bored by the whole situation, he turned his head and loped behind the cabin to disappear into the trees.

Whoosh. Blair didn't realize she'd been holding her breath until she expelled it. She'd seen the wolf before. That one and an older version that melted into the forest whenever she appeared. Apparently, they considered Mateo's property part of their territory. And speaking of which, where the hell was he?

She took an impatient step forward then faltered

as the hair on the back of her neck rose. The sense of a malevolent presence increased with the disappearance of the wolf. Her hand on the pistol at her waist, she whipped around and stared into the trees that surrounded the house. She appreciated Mateo's desire for privacy but did it have to be in the middle of bumfuck nowhere?

Blair considered herself a pragmatist and seldom gave way to flights of fancy. Still a ripple of unease stole over her like a thick, tangible mist smothering her senses. She drew her gun, forcing her hand not to tremble.

"Delaney."

She whirled. The sheriff stood on the porch shirtless and shoeless, worn jeans riding low on lean hips. Her heart gave a hard thump and her blood pooled at her feet. Dammit to hell, why couldn't she work for someone who was overweight, balding and ate too many donuts? Though, on the plus side, he did have a way of heating her up and keeping the chill at bay.

He took one swift glance at the gun and was off the porch and at her side in four long-legged strides. Even in the biting wind, heat poured off him.

"Aren't you cold?"

He ignored the question and cut to the heart of the matter. "What's wrong? Why is your gun drawn?"

Feeling like an idiot, she cleared her throat. With his appearance the malevolent sensation dissipated like smoke. "I thought someone was watching." She holstered her gun.

He took a step past her, alert, dangerous.

She put a hand on his arm. Warmth surged through her fingers. Motionless, his nostrils flared. She dropped her hand.

One heartbeat. Two. The dark closed in around her.

Then the tension in him vanished as quickly as it came.

"Whatever, whoever is gone."

"How do you know?" But she knew what his response would be. The same one it always was.

"Gut feeling." He shrugged.

A gut feeling that caused his nostrils to flare and draw in a heavy inhale as if he sniffed the air. She shrugged it off. She was too much a realist to give credence to 'gut feelings' but savvy enough not to argue about the sheriff's. Instead, got down to the matter at hand. "Don't worry about it. Something's come up."

He cast one long, last look into the deep, dark of the woods then turned his sharp gaze back to her. "What?" He raked fingers through thick, black hair sprinkled with silver. The beginnings of moonlight outlined damn fine pecs and a lean torso.

"We need to get to the rez."

"Not our jurisdiction." He started toward the house.

"The chief of police specifically requested you." She fell in step beside him. Demanded more like, but she wisely kept that to herself.

"Kipp? Jesse Kipp?" His eyebrows rose.

Blair strove for patience, not her strong suit, and managed not to roll her eyes. There was only one on the rez. "Yup."

"Why?"

They crossed the porch and he swung through the door.

She stepped in behind him and looked around. A small entryway led into a sparsely furnished, spacious living room with a large west window that always drew her. Pine and oak beckoned. And when the sun went down, it turned the whole landscape into a crimson and purple pallet of glory. But tonight, the view she loved made her feel vulnerable as the sky blackened and the branches reached out twisty, skeletal fingers. Impatient with herself, she pulled her mind back to the reason for being here.

"There's a little three-year-old girl that's lost. The weather is supposed to drop. Jesse needs all the help he can get."

He straightened. His strange amber-colored eyes flared. He gave an abrupt nod. "Give me two minutes."

"Mind if I grab a bottle of water?"

"Help yourself." He motioned behind him toward the kitchen as he disappeared into the bedroom.

Striding in, she blinked as shiny copper pans caught the artificial light when she flipped the wall switch. The kitchen, both small and sparse, gleamed. The only personal item, a dreamcatcher hanging from the ceiling in the corner whose feathers fluttered as the furnace kicked on. Mateo had done a four-year stint in the Marines right out of high school.

Apparently, the emphasis on order and sanitation stuck.

Three steps took her to the stainless-steel refrigerator, where she reached in and pulled out a bottle of water.

She'd barely uncapped it and taken a healthy gulp when Mateo appeared in the doorway with worn climbing boots on his feet, wearing a bomber jacket identical to hers and his badge on his belt.

"You ready?"

She capped the water and followed him out.

Bare branches slapping against the cabin's green metal roof made her jump. Once again a wolf bayed, throaty and challenging. She quickened her step to the dark SUV and opened the driver's door.

"I'll drive."

Of course you will. She tossed him the keys and headed for the passenger side. He caught them with one hand, climbed in and motored toward the reservation. "Where are we headed?"

"Do you know where Ed Cobel's farm is?"

"Bumps up against the base of the mountains? Yeah." He tapped the steering wheel with long restless fingers. "It's going to get cold tonight."

"It already is." She burrowed into her jacket and turned up the heat. It came out of the vent with a whoosh of warm air that had her tight muscles loosening.

"Your blood just hasn't thickened up, Southern girl." He pushed his foot on the gas and the SUV barreled forward.

She'd moved from the teeming city of Atlanta, Georgia two years ago to the little town of Grizzly, Montana, population 6,792 and seat of the county police department. Her first winter here, she was sure she'd freeze to death. Since then, she never really warmed up till June.

Glancing up she tensed, grabbed the dash and yelled, "Look out."

The lights illumed a six-point buck.

"I see him." He stomped on the brakes. Tires shrieked.

The buck crossed the road in one graceful leap. Blair released her grip on the dash then tightened it again as a doe bounded behind it. Mateo swerved to the left then back to the right, missing the doe by mere inches. Blair closed her eyes and blew out the air trapped in her lungs.

"It's always the females that cause the trouble." Mateo straightened the wheel.

"Excuse me? That's a sexist remark if I ever heard one." Her eyebrows soared as she shifted in the seat to face him.

"Just pushing your buttons, Delaney."

"Yeah, more like you probably had another fight with Jugsie."

This time his eyebrows went up. "Now who's making sexist remarks? Her name's Samantha, as you well know."

"Just calling a spade a spade or a jug a jug." She snorted at her own humor.

He shook his head. "With that Southern accent

you make the vilest things sound like honey dripping from your tongue. A Southern belle with a mouth of a trucker.

"We broke up. Not that we were really together."

"I'm not a Southern belle." That statement irritated more than the mouth of a trucker comment. The rest of what he said registered. "That's the fifth woman you've broken up with since I've been here. You need to move to the city. You live in too sparse an area to go through women at the rate you do. There will be none left for you to go out with."

"I don't believe in serious relationships. I make that clear when I first start dating."

She nearly snorted. Dating being a euphemism for getting them in the sack. The coffee gossip at the jail was he'd been in a pretty serious relationship several years back that had ended badly and rocked the small community with its intensity, both the relationship and the breakup. The woman was an unknown. She'd blown in from nowhere, spent most of her time at his place and blown out when the relationship ended.

"What about you. How's that long-distance romance going?" He glanced over at her then turned his eyes back to the road.

She shrugged. "Oh, just fine if you like phone sex."

He threw back his head and laughed. A full rich sound that reminded her of smooth malt whiskey. She cleared her throat and asked what was on the forefront of her mind. "Do you think we can get the child back?"

His hands tightened on the wheel and he looked

straight ahead. "We'll get her back."

She nodded. In some it might sound like braggadocio. But not coming from Mateo Grey. No one tracked like the sheriff. Not even the residents of the Blackfeet Nation where they were headed. And they were no slouches in the tracking department. He was nineteen for nineteen and that was just since she'd worked for him.

"Tell me what you know about the girl's disappearance."

She told him what she knew which wasn't that much. "They didn't know she was gone till this morning, when her mom went in to check on her."

Leaned over the wheel, he straightened. His body language and his facial features changed, became sharper, more intense. His unusual amber eyes glittered. A fission of unease traveled up her spine and lodged at the base of her neck. He looked angry and dangerous. Even though she knew it was directed at the situation not her, it shook her. But she'd be damned twice over before she let her boss know she sometimes found him intimidating.

"It was down to twenty degrees last night. And in the mountains even colder." He shifted restlessly in his seat. "Was she taken or just wandered off?"

She shrugged then realized he couldn't see her. "Don't know. There's no indication she was taken or that anyone outside the family was in the house."

They fell silent. Dark clouds traveling overhead made the indigo night even darker. The barren trees along the road threw the sheriff's face in and out of shadow adding to the eeriness of the drive. Her heart ached as she thought about a toddler alone in the cold and dark. Or was she?

Twenty minutes later they pulled into the Cobel's farm. A patrol car and trucks, some well maintained, some rusted, lined the road. Flashlights blinked in the dark as far as the eye could see like oversized fireflies.

Jesse Kipp, the Chief of Police on the rez walked toward them, his expression cautious. Medium height, he looked taller because of the way he carried himself.

Mateo swung out of the car. Blair jumped out and walked around the side at the same time that Jesse stopped in front of them. Jesse gave her a brief nod then turned his attention to Mateo. Neither man smiled.

"Mateo."

"Jesse. Any luck?"

The chief shook his head.

"Tell me where you've searched."

"The buildings, the fields and the base of the mountains."

"Do you think she was taken?"

"There's no signs of it, but we can't rule it out."

"She's the only one missing?"

"Her and the family dog."

"What kind of dog?" Mateo looked around as he spoke.

"Just a mutt. Some retriever in him."

"What's the little girl's name?"

"Mary."

"I'll need something of hers before we start searching."

"Why?"

"That's the way I work. You know that."

The chief of police studied him, shrugged then led the way into an old, two-story farmhouse that blazed with light, taking the steps that led to the porch two at a time.

"Mrs. Cobel." Mateo took the hand of a harried-looking woman with red, swollen eyes. Wisps of black hair had slipped out of a limp ponytail that hung in stringy streaks down her back.

"Sheriff, can you find my girl?"

"I'll do my best. Can you give me something that belongs to Mary?"

"Of course." She didn't bother to ask why, just hurried off. Minutes later she came back with a one-eyed, scraggly-looking teddy bear.

"Thank you." He took the teddy bear and gave her a reassuring smile.

For just a moment she smiled back.

Blair watched the exchange. He was gentle with her. Gentler than he was with most. She had no idea why he wanted the bear. It wasn't like they had a tracking dog. But inevitably he always wanted something that belonged to whoever was lost.

With a nod, he strode out the door. Blair lengthened her stride to keep up. They reached the porch and he stopped, the lamplight catching and highlighting the premature streaks of silver at his temple. Still holding the bear, he put his face in the wind and closed his eyes. He stood there, motionless.

The wind shifted. He opened his eyes and straightened. Jumping off the porch he headed west.

He skirted the barn and veered toward the mountains. Blair broke into a trot beside him. "Where are we going?"

"Into the foothills." He strode on, his expression intent, leaning into the wind.

"Why are we going in that direction?" She pumped her arms trying to ignore the sting of the wind on her face.

"Because that's where we are going to find the little girl."

"How do you know?" Her heart rate picked up as she struggled to keep up with legs considerably longer than hers.

He didn't answer. She hadn't expected him to.

He trudged toward the foothills.

"You think she went into the mountains?"

He turned and gave her an impatient look.

She shut up and followed him.

He scrambled up a half-formed trail to the right, shining his powerful mag light in front of him. The going steeper the farther they climbed. She followed kicking debris and sending pebbles tumbling in her wake as she bent over to leverage herself up the trail. She stumbled over a rough, large rock. Flinging out her arms, she righted herself.

They'd been at it nearly an hour when he stopped abruptly and she plowed into him. "Oof." It was like hitting a boulder. Every square inch of him muscled and hard. Frustration leached into the air.

"What's wrong?"

"Wrong direction. This is a dead end."

CHAPTER 2

"You're spooky."

She stood with hands fisted on her hips trying to ignore the woo-woo vibes he gave off. "You're sniffing the air like a dog who's lost the scent."

He didn't respond. Stood motionless, his nostrils flaring, his gaze roving, his body taut.

Blair's heart dropped. She'd tried to keep hope of finding this child tamped down. Even though it seemed impossible odds, no tracks, no clues, no leads, Mateo had found the missing before. She took a deep breath and straightened her spine. And something inside her insisted he would this time too, even if he did claim they were on a dead end.

Seconds became minutes. Night deepened. An occasional star winked diamond bright against an inky black sky. The chill in the air grew. The time they'd spent going in the wrong direction had cost them.

He motioned back the way they'd come. Went a hundred yards then veered east. Her heart rose from her toes to her knees as once again expectations began to flutter upward.

They traveled for another twenty minutes going

deeper into nearly impenetrable thickets, thorny and knurled, shadowy and dark in the moonlight.

"Ouch." She rubbed her cheek when a bramble slipped from her hand and struck her face. A sharp sting from cheek to jaw.

He whirled. "Are you all right?"

"Fine." The words were no sooner out than she stepped into a hole.

"Crap." Her foot twisted. Hot pain shot through her. She collapsed and grabbed her ankle.

He spun around, beside her in an instant. The scent of musk strong on his person. On a primitive level, something basic in her responded.

Ignoring it, she waved him away. "Go. Find the little girl."

He didn't answer, just yanked off her boot in one smooth motion that had her biting back a yelp.

"Mateo, go. Find the little girl before it's too late."

"Shut up, Chief Deputy." He didn't raise his voice, but no one argued with Mateo when he used that tone. She subsided, muttering under her breath, and winced when he pressed on bruised skin. His touch lightened and his fingers probed gently. An expression of relief tracked across his face then disappeared like the moon behind clouds. "Nothing's broken. You just strained it. You're tough for a Southern girl." He pushed her boot back on. Still squatting, he asked, "Do you want me to make you a walking stick or do you want to wait here?"

"Are we close?"

"Yes."

"If it won't cut far into our time, I'll take a walking stick."

He disappeared and she heard a crack. Moments later he was back, a long limb in hand. It was rough and had knobby edges but it would work. He pulled her to her feet, handed it to her, then spun on his heel.

Without a word he pushed forward, all his attention on something ahead that only he could see or sense, the teddy bear's head bobbing out of his pocket. She hobbled forward breathing heavily, sweating inside her jacket, determined not to slow him down. It had been her decision to come. She'd have to keep up and she knew it.

He stopped abruptly and turned his head listening.

Grateful, she leaned on the stick so caught up in regulating her breath it took her a moment to hear the distant bark.

A dog!

Her heart moved from her knees to her throat and thumped so hard she had problems swallowing. The Cobel's had a dog.

Mateo pushed forward.

The pain in her ankle increased. It seemed like they'd been on the move forever but she doubted if it had been more than ten minutes.

He thrust aside the underbrush and stopped. She bumped her nose into the hard bones of his shoulder. Rubbing it, she inched awkwardly around him.

Crouched in a small rocky indent, her arms wrapped around a large yellow dog, squatted a little girl. Seeing them, the dog laid his head on the ground, his attitude submissive. Dogs always had an odd response to Mateo. They either challenged him, were submissive or fearful.

She forgot about the dog and hobbled toward the child, barely aware of the shooting discomfort in her ankle.

"Are you alright, honey?" She bent down, studied the little tyke dressed in fuzzy torn jammies with feet in them. Her face scratched and dirty. The dog moved closer to the toddler and wrapped himself around her like she was a puppy.

"Cold. Hungry." The child's face screwed up as if about to cry.

"We'll get you home."

Mateo's jacket rustled as he tore it of and wrapped it around the tyke then scooped her up. He handed her the teddy, pressed her head into his shoulder to avoid the briars, and headed for the farm. Blair limped behind. The dog trailed Blair.

"You okay, Delaney?" He called over his shoulder.

"I'm good." Then added in a gruff voice as her heart swelled and her eyes filled. "You saved her, Mateo."

"The dog saved her. I suspect it was his body heat that kept her warm. I just found her."

"Deny as much as you want but you saved her."

Mary bobbed her head up. "I want my mommy." The child's lips trembled. Streaky tears glistened in the moonlight as she clutched her beloved teddy bear.

"You're a very brave girl, Mary. Can you hang on

just a little longer?" His voice gentle, he drew her close, sharing his body heat. If he was cold without his jacket, it didn't show.

Her head bobbled up and down. "Are you a doggy?"

Blair put her hand over her mouth to hide her snort of amusement and coughed instead.

"I'm the sheriff. Why do you ask?"

"You smell like a doggy. And you are very warm."

He gave a low chuckle. "I need a shower, don't I?"

Mary nodded.

Odd. Mateo always had a woodsy scent to him like crisp moonlit air and tree bark that was all male and very appealing. But the little girl was right, Mateo sometimes—like tonight—exuded an animal smell, a musky scent.

It didn't happen often. Mainly under times of stress, like missing persons or the time someone had pointed a gun at her and Mateo had disarmed him.

Hmm. She wondered what her stress pheromones smelled like and shrugged. Probably no better. She tried for a discreet sniff into her collar.

"Better call Jesse."

His voice brought her back to the matter at hand.

"Oh sh—shoot." For a moment, she'd forgotten the child. "I should have done that right away." She speed-dialed the chief, told him the good news and their location.

"Is she alright?" Jesse asked.

"Cold and hungry, but other than that, she appears okay."

"I'll tell her parents." The chief clicked off without

waiting for a response.

As Mateo shoved through the underbrush, she shone her mag in front of them trying to light the way.

"Want me to go first?" she asked as a branch slapped him in nearly the same spot she'd gotten scratched.

"Not necessary." He walked sidewise, kept the child protected and his head down. Even without free hands to push through the brush, he still set a pace she had problems keeping up with. He said nothing just stopped every few minutes for her to catch up.

Finally, he broke through the undergrowth and started down the rock slope.

Below flashlights waving in a stream of light, bobbed in their direction. Two figures broke ahead of the pack and raced toward them, their lights dipping and bobbing.

"Mary," Mrs. Cobel called.

"Mommy. Mommy," the child wailed.

In minutes, the little girl's parents reached them. Tears streaming down Mrs. Cobel's face, she snatched up her daughter and clutched the child to her. "My baby. Are you all right?"

"Hungry. I want to go home."

"Don't you worry, Mommy's here. I'll take care of you."

"She's alright?" she asked above the child's wails.

"Get a doctor to look her over but I think considering her adventure she is going to be fine. You might want to give that dog of yours an extra big soup bone. He stayed by her side and probably kept her from freezing."

"That dog is going to be treated like royalty for the rest of his life." She rocked her child, her hand pressing Mary's head to her shoulder.

"What about you two?" For the first time she noticed Blair leaning on the walking stick.

"I strained my ankle. I'm okay."

"Are you sure?" She cradled the child and swayed to and fro as she spoke.

"I'm sure."

"What can I do to thank you?"

He made a dismissive gesture with his hand. "Just glad we could find her."

Sensing the woman needed to do something to show her gratitude, Blair spoke up. "Mateo actually found her, but we both have a weakness for blackberry pie."

A huge smile crossed Mrs. Cobel's face, lifting worry lines and showing a genuinely pretty woman. "You've got it."

By now the rest of the searchers had reached them. Several slapped them on the back and congratulated them. The party trooped to the farm. As everyone headed for the house, Mateo and Blair strode to the car.

"Mateo." A voice called in the dark.

He turned.

Jesse Kipp stood a few feet away. "I owe you."

Mateo raised a hand in acknowledgement and jumped into the car. Blair limped to the other side where Mateo had thrown the door open. He grabbed her arm and pulled her up.

"Turn this beast on and get the heat going."

"You are such a Southern flower," he teased. The engine turned over and air whooshed out of the vents. Unfortunately, cold.

"Since that little girl still has your jacket you've got to be frozen."

She reached over and touched his cheek with her fingertip then nearly put her whole hand on his face to warm it.

"How can you not be cold?" Her eyebrows rose to her hairline.

"I'm hot blooded."

She snorted. "Either that or very sick. And I mean that in the best possible way."

"Huh."

The rest of the drive back to Mateo's cabin passed in relative silence. Blair concentrated on the painful thawing of her limbs and finding a comfortable position for her foot while Mateo concentrated on the road. The scanner quiet.

He wheeled the SUV into his long dirt lane. The light picked up a rabbit sitting in the center of the road. He slowed and it hopped to safety. Halting the big black cruiser in front of his cabin, he jumped out of the car. "Are you going to be okay? Can you drive home?"

"I only strained my ankle, Grey, not broke my leg. Plus, it's my left so there's no problem using the pedals. I'll see you tomorrow."

"By the time you get home and in bed, it will be

tomorrow. Put some ice on that ankle and get a few hours sleep."

"Yeah, will do." She hobbled around the car to the driver's side, since there was no room to slide over with all the paraphernalia on the dash and in the center of the seat. Before she could crawl in, he picked her up and tossed her in. For a moment her heart did a hard thump then settled. The heat from his hands as warm as if he'd touched bare skin.

He waved and strode to the porch.

She turned the cruiser and looked in the rearview mirror. Mateo stood watching her. The lamplight silhouetting his figure, throwing his shadow, long and lean, across the porch.

She raised a hand certain the distance was too far to be seen.

He lifted his in return.

Damn. The man had eyes like a cat. She took a deep inhale, letting her tired body relax and giving in just a little to the discomfort in her ankle. Mateo's intensely male scent of fresh air and forest lingered in the driver's seat. She gave an appreciative sniff. It was then she noticed the animal smell had disappeared.

~*~

The phone rang long, loud and accusing. At the same time, Quinn's voice boomed as he spoke into the dispatch radio. On top of the noise, the reek of stale coffee assaulted Mateo's sensitive olfactory receptor neurons as he stepped into the jail house. Thank Christ he'd had the sense to stop at Belle's Bean

Factory, the local coffee shop, and get a large coffee to go before he got to work.

Adam Brasher, his nineteen-year-old office assistant, looked up as he grabbed the phone and waved papers at Mateo. "Hello. No, he's not available. Give me the information and I'll see he gets it." He scribbled furiously on a note pad, hung up then handed it along with the paper to Mateo as he passed, heading for his office. "Morning, Boss. These need signed."

"How did that test go?"

Adam took night classes in the hope of one day becoming a lawyer. Though who the hell would want to be a lawyer was beyond Mateo's understanding. Still, he was a good kid and he admired the fact that Adam wanted hands-on experience with the law.

"Aced it."

Mateo gave a thumbs up.

Quinn's whiskey-rough voice barked into the radio. "What's that. Say again? Give me detes." Quinn, a grizzled sixty-year-old, spent his downtime at the local honky-tonk singing in a country western band and downing shots.

Mateo wasn't sure why he continued to work in the sheriff's office. His rough, raw voice drew crowds.

"Is Blair in yet?" He raised his voice to carry over Quinn's, who talked like he held a stage-mic in his hand.

Adam pointed.

Mateo turned in time to see Blair come through the door, not moving quite as briskly as she normally did but not limping either.

Adam handed him a pen.

Mateo glanced at the papers and started signing, not even making it to his desk.

"Bob's awake and bellowing to be let out." Adam nodded his head toward the cell.

Bob Older was a construction worker that worked his tail off Monday through Friday then let off steam on the weekends. Mateo was thinking about naming one of the two cells in the station in Bob's honor since he spent so much time there.

"If he's sober, let him out and tell him no more fights or tearing up Maddy's Place, for all the good it will do."

Adam grabbed the keys and took off with a jaunty step pushing his black-framed glasses back up to the bridge of his thin nose. Mateo knew he got tired of doing glorified secretarial work and would like to see a little more action but he never complained. If the kid wasn't so determined to become an attorney, he'd make a damn fine sheriff someday.

A whiff of sugar and yeast caused his nose to twitch. He turned slowly and noticed Delaney had a hand behind her back.

"You better have brought enough for everyone, Delaney."

The woman had tight muscles on a slender body devoid of fat and ate like a linebacker. How she did it, he'd never know.

She sighed and pulled out the brown bag that rustled as she opened it.

Quinn grabbed it as she walked by, took a couple and handed the bag back. He took a huge bite and swallowed. "You two might want to hear this."

Before Mateo could respond, Bob and Adam tromped out of the holding area. Bob's bleary eyes lit when he saw the donuts. "Hey, can I have one of those?"

"I'm not going to reward you for bad behavior." Delaney's eyebrows beetled together and her lips thinned.

"Aw, come on, Blair. That's just downright mean." Bob wheedled.

She glanced at Mateo, saw his twitching lips and threw the sack on the dispatcher's desk. "Fine."

As if afraid she'd change her mind, Bob grabbed one.

"Now get out of here."

"Thanks, Blair." He shoved through the door.

"That's Chief Deputy Delaney to you," she called to his retreating form. "No one takes me seriously around here," she muttered. She whirled around to find the three men busy biting back smiles. "What?" Her fists went to her hips.

"Nothing." Mateo threw his hands in the air.

Adam grabbed the signed paper work and disappeared behind the desk.

"Honey," Quinn said in his gravel-rough voice. "The folks that have seen you toss a man twice your size to the ground and cuff him, take you plenty serious."

"That's true." She nodded, mollified.

"Now you all need to listen up." Quinn's voice boomed.

"What've we got, Quinn?" Mateo strode over and leaned on the desk.

"Caulfield's prize bull got attacked early this morning. Opel thought she heard something, and instead of waking George, went out to check on it and got attacked too."

"Someone attacked the bull and then accosted her?" Mateo straightened.

Quinn shrugged. "They sliced the bull then slugged her. George woke up and when Opel wasn't there, he went looking for her. Saw what was happening and fired a shot in the air. The intruder took off."

"And they're just now calling?" Blair's brows shot up.

"Actually, Rose called it in. She was out there earlier and took a statement but knew Mateo would want to talk to them in person.

"Instead of calling the station, Opel called Rose on her cell."

"Rose is just now calling it in, instead of when it happened?" The sheriff frowned.

Deputy Rose DeWitt was forty something, carried too much weight and had a heart of gold. The good will between the county and the sheriff's department could be laid directly at Rose's feet. And a good thing too, since he was up for re-election.

"Come on, Sheriff. You know Rose. If it was something she couldn't handle, she would have called you, but she knew you two were up at all hours hunting that Cobel kid. Heard on the scanner you found her."

"Yeah. We got lucky." He appreciated Rose's thoughtful side. Still, she should have called him sooner.

Quinn snorted. "With your kind of luck at tracking, you should buy a lottery ticket. Hell, buy me one too."

Mateo grunted, grabbed his coffee that he hadn't had a chance to drink and headed for the door. "You coming, Delaney?"

She seized her donuts and followed him.

"Blair." Adam eyed the donut sack, his voice plaintive.

She rolled her eyes and tossed him the sack. "That's Chief Deputy Delaney to you."

He caught the sack. "Thanks, Chief Deputy Delaney."

She shook her head and hurried through the door. Only limping slightly. "So, who would slash up a prize bull and slug Opel?"

Mateo hopped into the big SUV parked squarely in front of the police station and turned over the motor.

Blair slid into the passenger side. "Want me to drive?"

"Nope."

"So, who would slash up a prize bull then pop Opel?" She asked again as she lifted her leg, moving her foot to get comfortable and stuck it out in front of her.

He threw her a glance. "Ankle still bothering you?"

"Not a bit."

He snorted but let it go.

"Well?" She prodded.

"Sounds like someone with a vendetta."

"With the Caulfields? Nobody's got a bad thing to say about them from here to the next six counties."

She sniffed and her eyes arrowed to his cup. "Can I have some of your coffee?"

In response, he took a sharp right and pulled into the fast food on the corner. Going through the drive up he ordered a large coffee and four egg and bacon biscuits.

Blair brightened.

In minutes they were back on the road. As soon as they were out of town, he put his foot on the gas. The first stubble of frost-covered prairie grass flew by. He glanced at his watch. Eight o'clock. In another two hours the frost would be melted. They were just lucky it wasn't snow.

The bag rustled as he reached in. "So how does that phone thing with your boyfriend work?" he asked around a mouthful of biscuit.

"Seriously?"

"I've never had a long-distance relationship."

"Think webcams."

"Huh. Does that do it for you?"

"Well. It's certainly not like up close and personal. You volunteering, Mateo?"

His hand jerked the wheel, careening them into the other lane where an oncoming truck driver laid on his horn. Mateo got back in his lane with inches to spare.

Blair patted the front of her blouse where the coffee she'd been holding arced out of her cup and landed. "It was a joke."

"Sometimes your I'm-just-one-of-the-boys attitude gets annoying," he muttered, his face heating.

"So, who else has been propositioning you? Quinn or Adam?"

"Give it a rest, Delaney."

She took one look at his face, opened her mouth and promptly shut it.

Mateo fought the overwhelming urge to bang his head against the steering wheel and howl, embarrassed frustration churning his belly. She had certainly had a laugh at his expense. It had been mainly his fault. What was he thinking? Why did they always have these sexually charged conversations? At the very least, it was unprofessional. Not to mention downright dangerous. Putting the moves on his chief deputy would be the biggest mistake of his career.

He made no attempt at further conversation and neither did she. Half an hour later, he wheeled onto the Caulfield's ranch.

As he turned off the engine, and hopped out, Opel's husband stepped out of the barn and strode toward them. A bowlegged, short man wearing worn jeans, an old red flannel shirt and a jean jacket. "Sheriff." George held out his hand.

Mateo clasped it. "George. Want to tell me what

happened?"

"Someone slashed up our prize bull then when Opel showed up, slugged her. Craziest thing. Why would anybody do that? If I hadn't shown up when I did and let loose some buckshot, I don't know what would have happened." He ran restless fingers through short graying hair.

"Have you or Opel made any enemies?" Mateo rocked on his heels and studied the older man in front of him.

George snorted then tugged on his ear. "I guess it's possible for me. Though I can't think of anyone off the top of my head. But Opel? You know she mothers everyone in this county and the surrounding ones. Comes from us never having any children I guess." He looked into the distance as if after all these years, the idea still hurt. He refocused on Mateo. "Why don't I show you the bull then you can talk to Opel."

He motioned toward the barn. They walked behind him to a large holding pen. "I'd put the bull in here. I was getting ready to breed him."

With Blair at his heels, Mateo walked forward and squatted to study the bull. It had been senselessly savaged. "I thought Opel said a man attacked her. This looks like an animal attack."

"I know it." He scratched his head. "She didn't see any animal, just walked into a fist."

"In the pen or out?"

"Out, under that grove of trees." George pointed to a stand of oak.

Mateo studied the trees, near enough to the pen

to provide shade then turned his attention back to the dead bull. Its throat had been ripped out and long jagged tears made along its belly and legs.

He sniffed. His hackles rose. The scent of wolf, a distinctive men's cologne, leather and the illusive scent of woman filled his nostrils. And lacing it all, the thick malevolent smell of evil.

CHAPTER 3

It clung to his nostrils and filled his pores. Bile pushed up from his stomach and lodged in his throat. What the hell had come to his territory?

"Are you alright?" The blue in Delaney's eyes always deepened when she grew concerned and icy when angry.

Right now, they headed toward violet and managed to right his spinning world.

Pushing to his feet, he dusted his hands. "Fine. Let's talk to Opel."

"She's still a little shaky, Sheriff." George warned, clearly fretting about his wife.

"I'll do my best not to upset her."

Mateo and Blair slipped through the rails of the enclosure while George let himself out the gate. They tromped to the house and onto the porch where two bright blue rocking chairs sat side by side. The paint on the arms worn. A decorative rust-colored star on the wall behind. The porch was much like the couple, Mateo mused, clean, neat and frayed around the edges.

George opened the door. "Opel," he called out.

"In the kitchen."

As they approached, the aroma of fresh coffee and

hot apple pie wafted toward them.

Mateo's stomach growled.

Blair started to laugh then hers followed suit.

Mateo grinned.

She shrugged and rubbed her hands together. Opel's apple pies were the best in the county.

"She bakes when she's upset or nervous." George lengthened his stride and went into the kitchen ahead of them. He put his hand on his wife's shoulder. "We got company, hon. The sheriff and his deputy are here."

"Good thing I baked a pie and put the coffee on, isn't it?" She turned from the oven, wiping her hands on a spotless, white apron. A dark bruise purpled her jaw.

Mateo clenched his teeth. Anger erupted. He pushed it down, hard. He'd been in law enforcement since he was twenty-two. He knew what people could do to one another. But hitting a woman old enough to be his grandmother didn't set well. Not at all, especially in his territory.

"George not like your meat loaf, Opel?" Instead of letting the outrage show, he teased her.

George stiffened.

"The sheriff's joking. It's just his way." She smiled and patted her husband's cheek.

"Some joke," her husband grumbled.

"Have you put any ice on that?" Blair stepped forward and took Opel's hand.

For some reason, a gentle Blair always surprised Mateo. She was one of the toughest females he knew and never backed down on anything. But everybody in the county loved Opel. Blair no exception.

"Now, don't go fussing over me, Blair dear. I'm perfectly fine."

"Why don't you sit down and tell us what happened." Blair's voice pure Southern honey.

"Let me pour you some coffee and get you a piece of pie, then I'll tell you all that I know, which isn't much more than what I told Rose."

Chairs scraped as Blair and Mateo sat down.

George poured coffee and Opel placed large slabs of pie in front of them.

Mateo finished his off in four bites, took a slug of his coffee and set the mug down. "So, what happened, Opel?"

She'd been moving the pie around on her plate but made no attempt to eat. Straightening her shoulders, she folded her hands in her lap. "I always leave the window cracked a little in the bedroom. I like the fresh air and listening to the wildlife. That's when I heard Blue. The bull. He sounded panicked. I hopped out of bed. I didn't want to wake George. He'd had a full day, so I grabbed the ball bat that we keep at the foot of the bed and headed out. By the time I got near the pen, Blue was screaming. She plucked at her apron and her face fell in folds of distress. "When I got there he was gone. Savaged. Ripped apart."

She made a valiant effort to pull herself together. "I saw movement in the trees so I went to investigate."

Mateo cleared his throat and opened his mouth.

"I know, Sheriff. George has mentioned it a

thousand times today and quite frankly I'm tired of hearing it. I know I behaved foolishly. But I was so angry. Killing that bull was senseless."

"Opel, no one I know would ever call you foolish, maybe just a little too fearless," Blair said.

Opel smiled at that and relaxed a bit.

"So, what happened next?" Mateo prompted.

"I ran into the woods, yelling and brandishing my bat and ran right into a fist. That's all I remember, till George found me."

Blair leaned forward. "How long was that, Mr. Caulfield?"

"Not long. I heard Opel yelling like a banshee, tossed on my pants and boots, grabbed my shotgun and took off. I swear her screams turned my blood cold. I fired a shot in the air and when I got there, it's like she said. She was out cold. Whatever it was, the shot must have scared it off." He shook his head.

"You know that bull looks like an animal mauled him. A wolf or bear." Mateo circled his empty mug on the table. He'd smelled wolf.

"It does at that. But I know a fist when I run into it." She sat down the coffee, she'd just brought to her mouth, untouched. "Though, the hand was hairy, almost furry. And hot."

Scents of a man or woman and scents of a wolf. He didn't like where his thoughts were going.

"Did you see anyone or anything before you were hit? A flash of skin. A glitter of eyes?"

She started to shake her head then caught herself. "He must have been dressed in black. Maybe wore a hoodie. I didn't even see the fist just felt it, but before I went down, I saw a glitter of eyes. Looked a lot like yours. Oh, not the color. These were bright as emeralds, not that unusual shade of amber like yours. But they had the same gleam to them yours get when you're worked up. Shiny-like. And the same slant."

His eyebrows went up, along with the hair on his neck.

"I'm sorry, Sheriff, I should have said distinctive."

"Don't worry about it. You aren't the first person that's commented on their color. You said he. What makes you think it was a male?"

"Just an assumption. I guess it could have been a female." She pushed back a gray hair, her expression saying she doubted it.

He shoved back his chair. "Thanks. You've been a big help. I'll have Rose take a turn or two through here for the next couple of nights. Blair's right. You need to ice that jaw."

"I'll see she does." George's chair scraped against the floor as he stood up.

The women followed suit.

Mateo shook hands with both George and Opel and headed out. He called over his shoulder, "I'll let you know what I find out."

As they stepped into the large SUV, Blair asked, "What the hell's going on? No human could have torn out that bull's throat like that."

"You wouldn't think so." He turned on the engine and backed up the truck.

"How would it be possible?"

"Serrated knife maybe or a person with a dog."

"Maybe." She leaned back in the seat. "What's the next step?"

"Like I said, I'll have Rose do a couple drive-bys. And have Quinn and Adam do some follow-up calls, see if there's been anything like this reported in any of the other counties. You can contact Jesse. You seem on good terms." He kept his voice casual, unsure why that irritated him.

"Went to the Blue Coyote, on the rez one night. Drank him under the table. He's been an admirer ever since." She smiled smugly.

Before he could respond, Quinn's voice came through the radio. "Sheriff. Just got a call from Randy Wiese. Seems he was out rabbit hunting, at least rabbits is all he's claiming, and a wolf killed his hunting dog and some deer. He saw it."

Mateo picked up the receiver. His blood quickened. A sense of dread slicked his skin.

"What in the several rings of hell is going on here?" Blair threw a hand in the air.

"Where's he now?" Mateo asked.

"In that track of woods behind his place."

"We just left the Caulfield place. We'll swing by. Over and out."

He twisted the wheel to the left and they bounced down a dirt road lined with pine.

Blair grabbed the side of the cab and hung on. "Since the Caulfield land borders Wiese's sounds like your wolfman has stayed in the area."

Mateo threw her a quick look and hit a pot hole

that caused her head to bounce off the ceiling.

"Dammit, Mateo." She rubbed her head.

"Why do you call him a wolfman?"

"Isn't it obvious?"

"Enlighten me."

"Kills like a wolf. Hits like a man. Ergo, wolfman."

"You don't believe that stuff, do you?" His voice even, his pulse thundered in his ears.

She shrugged. "I never rule anything out. It's what makes me such a good chief deputy." She winked at him.

"Doesn't sound like the pragmatist we all know and love."

"Maybe you don't know me as well as you think you do." She stared straight ahead.

He gave her a sidelong look. "Maybe I don't."

"Looks like Randy is waiting for us." She pointed.

A tall, gangly man dressed in camo green stood alongside the road in a stand of pine. "What do you want to bet he was trying to bag deer or elk out of season?"

"Sounds like a sucker bet." He maneuvered the SUV to the side of the road a few feet from where Randy stood, threw it in park and cut the motor.

They stepped out of the truck.

"Randy." Mateo nodded as he and Blair approached the hunter.

"Sheriff." His rifle cradled in his arm, Randy strode to meet them.

"What happened?"

"Damn wolf killed my best hound and a couple of

deer."

"How do you know it was a wolf?"

"I saw its bushy black butt."

"A black wolf. Rare in these parts. Sure, it wasn't gray?"

"Black."

Icy fingers skittered down his spine. It had been several years since he'd seen a black wolf. There'd been senseless carnage then too. "Tell us what happened."

"Was out hunting rabbits." His eyes shifted. "The dog smelled something. Started baying and took off. By the time I got there, there was two dead deer and the dog was down. His throat ripped."

"Better show us."

Randy motioned with his finger and trooped off through tall Ponderosa and Western Yellow Pine. The yellow-colored bark on the conifers gave off a pleasant vanilla scent that blended with the earthy aroma of the forest floor and helped notch down Mateo's tension.

"Don't wolves run in packs?" Blair pushed a low hanging branch out of the way before it slapped her in the face.

"Maybe it's one of those hybrid wolfdogs that old man Stone breeds," Randy volunteered.

"I heard he bred wolfdogs. Why?" Blair lengthened her stride to pull alongside Randy, pine cones crunching under her worn, sturdy boots.

"He gets nearly a thousand a head for them. Though why anyone would want a wolf for a pet is beyond me." Randy shook his head. "Are you going to check him out?"

"We will definitely talk to him." Blair promised.

They pushed their way through the underbrush and trees for another quarter mile till they came to a clearing. Two deer lay dead, along with the hound. All had been savaged.

Mateo knelt by the bodies and studied them. They had the markings of an animal attack along with the strong scent of wolf. He closed his eyes and took a deep inhale. Again buried under the wolf, the scent of woman, leather and men's cologne. Keeping his face impassive, he pushed up and walked around the clearing, following the scent then stopping when he saw tracks on the ground.

"You're right. One wolf."

"Told ya."

"How can you tell?" Blair looked around.

He pointed at the tracks. "It's a wolf alright. Small to medium. Small to be doing so much damage."

"What do you mean by that?" Randy demanded. "Has that wolf struck anywhere else?"

"Don't worry about it, Randy. We'll take care of it."

"You better," Randy blustered. "That was my best hunting dog."

"We'll be in touch. Let's go, Blair."

On the way back to town, she drummed her fingers on the dashboard. "What do you make of this? Opel shows us a bull that had been killed the same way as the deer, only she says she was attacked by a man. And Randy swears he saw the back end of a wolf. Do you think there's some crazy out there siccing his dog on animals?"

"There weren't any human tracks." Just the lingering smell.

"Maybe he was further away."

"Maybe."

"Another thing." The rhythm of her fingers picked up. "There weren't pieces torn from the animals. This wasn't about food."

CHAPTER 4

Blair rubbed her hands together in anticipation of a cold brew.

Wearing black skinny jeans and a white fitted tee, she stepped into one of Grizzly's two honky-tonks. Peanut shells crunched under boots and the yeasty scent of beer had her whistling off-key as she made her way to the bar. A song about whiskey and a hard-hearted woman wailed in the background. The tension knotting her neck and shoulders loosened. It wasn't like the cop bar she frequented when she was on the force in Atlanta but it had its own unique flavor. One she'd gotten into the rhythm of, the spirit of.

She slid in next to Quinn. It'd been one hell of a day. "How's Leroy doing?"

Leroy was the night dispatcher and the antithesis of Quinn, quiet and bookish. Though they were both close in age.

Quinn snorted and brooded into his beer. "He's been sniffing after Rose."

She bit back a smile. Everyone except Rose knew that Quinn Neely was either in love with her or at the least had a king-sized crush.

"You could always ask her out yourself."

He gave her a horrified look. "You don't screw around with a woman like Rose. She'd expect me to marry her."

The bartender, a big man with a bald head and a walrus mustache, strolled over. "The usual, Blair?"

She nodded then turned back to Quinn. "Would that be so bad?"

"She'd expect me to quit drinking and start going to church on Sundays. I'm not sure which would be worse."

Biting her lips and swallowing a smile, she gave him a commiserating pat on the back.

"He's just her type. Sober and saintly."

This time she couldn't hold back and laughed out loud. "Don't you think saintly might be pushing it a bit?"

Before he could respond, the band tuned up. A middle-aged man with a white cowboy hat and a red and black plaid, flannel shirt motioned to Quinn.

"Looks like I'm up."

Quinn had a small band that was popular with the locals. He had a whiskey, cigarette-rough voice that straddled between raspy and crooner. He sang both country and classic rock. Clumping on stage, he started out with a hard-hitting oldie, with a lot of drum and guitar, that had half the audience heading for the dance floor and the other clapping their hands.

"Here ya go, Blair." The bartender plopped a glass of golden liquid down. Foam rose then settled, not a drop spilled.

"Thanks, Levi."

"Hey, Blair." Jeremy Haskins, the owner, editor and reporter of the local newspaper *The Bear* dropped onto the stool Quinn had just vacated.

"Hello, Jeremy," she yelled over the sound of a steel guitar.

"So, what's the deal on the animal killings," he yelled back.

"For once, couldn't you just sit down and buy me a brew instead of haranguing me for news?"

"Levi, a beer for me and another for Blair." He leaned over the counter and yelled before turning back to her. "Looking good by the way." His gaze swept her, lingered on her breasts then returned to her eyes. He grinned.

"Okay, Haskins, what do you want besides my fine self?" Blair twirled her glass, leaving condensation circles on the bar. With thick black hair that accentuated a thin face, he wasn't bad looking. They'd even went out once, but nothing clicked. She wondered how much that lack of interest on her part had to do with her enigmatic boss. He had to be the only single male in Grizzly past puberty and under eighty who hadn't tried to put the moves on her. Was it because she worked for him or was there more to it? He certainly trash-talked on a regular basis.

Jeremy waved a hand in front of her face. "Earth to Blair."

"I heard ya."

"Then what's your response?"

"About?"

"Come on, Blair, don't be coy. The animal killings." He pulled a notebook with a worn green cover out of his pocket and reached for his pen.

"Haskins, stay off the police scanner and get a life." She shook her head.

"So, you think it's a wolfman?" He leaned toward her, his eyes gleaming. Her body tightened and she forced back a startled jerk. How did he know about that? Had she inadvertently said something over the scanner. She'd been joking—for the most part.

She forced a laugh. "Seriously, Haskins?"

"Human fist. Fangs? Come on talk to me, Blair."

She downed half her beer and slammed it on the bar. "Sorry, I'm not into conspiracy theories or little green men. Just here for the beer. But I'll dance with you." She jerked him off his stool. Her weak ankle a distant memory.

He stumbled after her.

After several songs, including a line dance, they left the floor hot and sweaty.

"Come on, give me something, Blair."

"No comment." She should have known better if she thought that she'd sidetracked the local newspaper owner.

"Well that's hardly a headliner."

She slugged down the rest of her now warm beer. "If this is your headliner, *The Bear*'s in trouble."

"Well I guess I could always go with Josiah getting drunk and driving Mac Ellison's truck home instead of his own." He gave her an infectious grin.

"Why you people insist on not only leaving your

vehicles unlocked but the keys in as well is something I'll never understand." She grumbled, shaking her head.

"Spoken like a true city girl. Now tell me what happened?"

She gave an exaggerated sigh. "Looks like a lone wolf killed George Caulfield's prize bull then took out Randy Wiese's prized hound."

"And the fist that slammed into Opel?"

"I'd like to hear the answer to that one too." The voice came from over her shoulder.

Blair's stomach dropped and acid spurted. For a moment her fists clenched before she relaxed then turned with her most Southern fake smile to face Mateo's opponent for the sheriff's seat, Alistair Etheridge, the senator's son. "Why hello, Alistair. Are you out slumming?"

~*~

While Blair poured on the charm instead of slugging the smug, sanctimonious, oily, glad-handing politician as she longed to, ten miles away Mateo stood on his porch, hands in back pockets studying the full moon that streamed an iridescent light on his private domain. He tilted his head and listened to a thousand night sounds: the wind sighing, mice scurrying, an owl hooting and the clicking of a few hearty insects.

He sniffed the air and smelled nothing out of the ordinary, just the sharp pungent odor of pine and loamy earth. The only carnivorous mammal, that of the old gray wolf that considered Mateo's forty acres his hunting grounds. And rightly so. It had been his before it had been Mateo's.

His mind drifted back to the day's unsettling events and the underlying scent of woman and evil. The illusive smell reminiscent of a scent he hadn't smelled in four years. A growl escaped his throat. It couldn't be. He'd warned her what would happen if she ever came back. He had to be misremembering the scent. Plus, there was the man's cologne. And the illusive scent of male mixed with leather. He let out a long breath. To find what had slaughtered the animals in this small community and attacked Opel, he'd have to go back to the Caulfield's.

It was a good fifteen miles from his place but he loved nothing better than a righteous, night run. Yearned for it in fact. Making up his mind, he tromped into the house and to the bedroom where he shucked his clothes. He stepped out the back door without a stitch on and thought about the animal inside.

He'd made the change so often there was no longer any discomfort or pain. The wolf came to the forefront, taking over. His bones reshaped and took form as he dropped to all fours. Fur sprouted on his body, his hands and feet now paws. His vision clear, his snout extended, he gazed at his surroundings from the glittering amber eyes of a large, gray wolf. Filled with the night and the joy of being, he threw back his head and howled. The old gray wolf answered.

Mateo took off running, the old wolf joining.

They loped side by side. When they reached Mateo's property line, the old wolf stopped. Mateo sniffed and nuzzled him a moment then headed on.

He stretched out his legs as far as they would go and raced the wind singing in his ears. Half an hour later, he arrived at Caulfield's. He skidded to a halt and approached cautiously. The problem with his plan —even though wolves weren't in season, the attacks were going to make everyone trigger happy and he'd just as soon not get shot in either human or animal form. Sniffing the air, he slunk forward. He needed to get to the grove of trees where Opel was attacked and the pen where the bull was killed.

The cattle in the pasture behind the barn began to shuffle and low. He slunk downwind and edged closer to the pen. Smells had grown fainter than they were this morning. Nose to the ground, he continued around the pen looking for a point of entry, dirt dug up where a wolf might have dug its way under.

Nothing.

He burrowed beneath the fence on the side farthest from the house and nosed around, sniffing as the moon traveled in and out of clouds. He'd waited till Opel and George would be asleep to make his reconnaissance.

He opened his mouth panting, trying to get more scent. It confused him. When he was in wolf form, he smelled only of wolf. When he was in human form and the wolf clawed to get out, he gave off the musky odor of man and wolf. He assumed it was true of all shifters.

He was the only shapeshifter in the area, if you discounted the old wolf, who now remained in wolf form a hundred percent of the time. Four years ago, there had been another, but he'd run her off and told her never to return. Now, the mixed scent was back, something he hadn't smelled in four years: wolf and the salty scent of woman. And mixed in, the pungent scent of male cologne and leather. Not separate scents but all rolled together in a confusing mix. He stood still, puzzling.

The moon chose that moment to drift away from the ponderous dark cloud it traveled behind, lighting the night. Time to move. This was no place he wanted to be caught in. He'd try to track the scent from the other side of the enclosure.

His paws thrust out, he bellied under the fence and pulled himself up.

Bang. The shot deafened. A searing pain grazed his front leg.

CHAPTER 5

Blair strode into the station wearing aviator shades and a scowl. Her head pounded. The smallest sounds magnified to shrieking proportions. This was all Mateo's fault. She'd entered into a drinking competition with Jeremy and accepted a date with oily Alistair to keep any flying buffalo dung from collecting on their fearless leader during his run for reelection.

She dropped into her chair and grabbed her head.

Quinn and Adam stared at her, grinning.

Her mouth opened to growl a response but all that came out, a puny moan.

Quinn pushed himself out of the dispatcher's chair, stretched and ambled over to the coffee pot where he poured a cup of black coffee into a mug that read "Dispatchers Tell the Police Where to Go", grabbed a bottle of water from the small fridge next to the sink then meandered over to her desk and thumped them down in front of her.

She winced and nodded her thanks.

"So, who'd you end up going home with? The nosy reporter or the slimy politician that's running against the sheriff? And if it's the politician I hope you rung him dry on what his campaign plans are."

"Neither. I'm in a relationship. Remember?" She ignored the coffee, uncapped the water and drank it straight down.

She took a deep breath. When she exhaled, a belch escaped.

"Feel better?" Quinn asked, his lips twitching.

"Marginally." She did a sweep of the austere room. Careful not to move her head too quickly. No Mateo. She frowned.

"Is he in his office?"

"He's not in yet," Adam replied still chewing a grin at her discomfort. At nineteen, partying was something he could relate to.

Her eyebrows shot up, causing her to wince again. Mateo was always the first one in. "Has anyone talked to him?"

Both men shook their heads.

"Don't you find that a bit odd?"

"Maybe he got luckier than you did." Quinn smirked.

Adam tittered.

Her headache that had receded with the water came roaring back. An unbidden image of a tight butt moving like pistons over a faceless female, and strong forearms bedewed with sweat, rose in her mind.

What in the world had brought that on? He was her boss for cripe's sake. Plus, she had a boyfriend. Something it seemed she had to remind herself of with more and more frequency.

Before she could respond, the bell over the door

jangled and Mateo came strolling in, his left arm in a sling.

"What the hell happened to you?" she demanded.

"Poacher on the property."

"Who?" Quinn asked, his eyes glittering with surprise or curiosity. With Quinn one never knew.

"Have no idea. He got away."

"He got away?" Three voices echoed with varying degrees of astonishment.

"That's right." He grabbed the papers Adam held up and disappeared into his office.

Blair rolled her fingers on the desk, her spidey sense on high alert. She was a pragmatist and believed black was black and white was white, but she also strongly believed in her spidey sagaciousness too. Maybe that didn't make sense, but who said it had to.

She sipped her coffee then pushed away from her desk. Adam had obviously made it. His coffee wasn't half bad. Quinn's was strong enough to turn a zombie human.

She poured another cup, veered toward Mateo's office and slipped on a wet spot on the floor near the coffee pot. "Damn this cheap ass, slick as snot, cement floor and damn our even cheaper congressmen. And damn—oh forget it." She thumped the cups down, sloshing more hot liquid. Shaking her burned hand, she picked up Mateo's cup and let herself in without knocking.

Mateo looked up then went back to the papers that were piled in front of him. "Make yourself at home, Delaney."

Instead of plopping down the cup like she normally would, she carefully sat it in front of him and eased into the scarred, wooden straight-back across from the desk.

He raised the cup. "Adam or Quinn?" Then sniffed. "Adam. Thanks. Just what I needed. I didn't stop at Belle's this morning." He closed his eyes and savored the aromatic caffeine before taking a healthy swallow. As he set the cup down, Quinn thumped on the door and stepped in.

"George just called. He said a gray wolf was hanging around the pen last night that his bull had been savaged in."

Mateo lifted one eyebrow but said nothing.

"He shot and hit it, but it managed to get away. He followed the blood trail for a short distance once the sun broke. It was headed in your direction then he lost the trail."

"Okay. Thanks, Quinn."

Quinn lifted his hand and let the door thump shut behind him.

Blair tilted the chair back till it balanced on two legs and looked pointedly at his arm.

"What?" He scowled his irritation.

"Nothing."

"Fine. Did you come here for any other reason than to bring me a cup of coffee? If it's the latter, I have it now and you can get on your own stack of paperwork."

He scanned the top sheet, signed it and set it to the side.

"Wouldn't it have been interesting if it was George who shot you?" She meant it as a joke but it was coincidental. A poacher shoots the sheriff, which had to be a first. No one got the drop on Mateo. And George shot a wolf about the same time.

"Do I look like a wolf to you, Deputy Chief Delaney?"

One thing she'd learned about Mateo, whenever he was hiding something he fell back on sarcasm, usually with enough bite to it to end the conversation.

"Yeah, sometimes." The words were out before she could pull them back, taking them both by surprise.

His unusual eyes, so wolf-like in shape and color, widened then narrowed. He opened his mouth to respond, but before he could, Adam tapped on the door and stuck his head in. "Phone call."

Mateo reached for the phone.

"It's for Blair, Sheriff."

Mateo pushed the phone over to her.

Blair reached for it.

Adam cleared his throat. "You might want to take it at your desk."

"Why is that?" Mateo turned his piercing stare on Adam.

"Who is it?" Her brow shot up.

"Detective Hanigan."

"Sh—Crap. I was supposed to call him last night."

For the first time, Mateo's laser gaze zeroed in on her pasty complexion and the dark circles that ringed her eyes. "You must have been at the Swing and Stomp most of the night." He arched a brow. Then reached for the stack of papers requiring his perusal and signature. "Just remember you're on the clock."

"I wasn't last night," she snapped and forced herself not to grab her pounding head.

"Well, you are now," he replied calmly, never looking up.

She would have stamped out but figured it would only make the headache worse so she crept through the door and started to close it behind her when a thought struck her. "You don't think it's one of those gray wolves that hangs around your property, do you?"

His head jerked up. He rubbed his chin as if considering her words. "Definitely not the old one and I'd be surprised if the young one would roam that far, but I'll certainly check it out." She nodded and slipped out of his office, surprised he hadn't thought of that himself.

Sliding into her chair, she picked up the phone, knowing both Adam and Quinn, who were busy moving things around on their desks, had their ears peeled. Men. They were nosier than women ever thought of being.

"Hello."

"Hey, babe."

"Hey yourself."

She noticed the door to the Sheriff's office open a crack and rolled her eyes.

"I was worried about you. You were supposed to call last night."

"I'm sorry. I got tied up. Police business."

Quinn let out a guffaw that he managed to turn into a cough.

She shot him a look then turned her attention back to the phone.

"What was that?" Luke asked.

"Quinn. He shoved a whole donut into his mouth and choked."

This time the snort came from the direction of the Sheriff's office. He was right. This was no place to conduct personal business.

"I'd eat you up just like that little ole donut if you were here right now."

"Sounds great, but I'm not. I'm at work." Good grief. It wasn't the time or place.

"Did you ask for some time off?"

"No. We're pretty busy right now."

Adam and Quinn's heads shot up at that.

"I guess I'll just have to come and see you."

The phone dropped from her nerveless fingers.

~*~

Mateo's hearing while acute wasn't quite good enough to hear what Delaney's boyfriend was saying, but he did hear the phone drop from her hand and a squawking on the other end followed by Delaney's breathless, "Sorry, Luke, I've got an incoming." And a clear click.

He forced his mind back to work and away from the irritating subject of Delaney's love life. Though the pictures it conjured, of her end of it, had him squirming in his seat and cursing under his breath.

Forcing his mind to matters at hand, he worked his way through the stack of papers.

The rest of the day passed uneventfully, except for the posters of smarmy Alistair Etheridge plastered in every building he went in, nailing him with an oily smile.

Preoccupied, he headed home, determined to find Opel's assailant. His sense of smell while keen in either form was best as the wolf's. He waited till sundown then headed out, his arm already healed. This time he approached the woods by Wiese's property cautiously, very cautiously. Wiese was a poacher.

He loped to where the dog and deer had been slain and growled in frustration. The smell was faint, but the same as at the Caulfield's ranch. He opened his mouth to catch scent just as the first fat raindrop plopped on his nose, making him growl in frustration. He'd never find the trail now.

As he sniffed the ground, a wolf screamed in terror and pain.

He stretched his legs and ran toward the torturous cries. Almost there, a green light bobbed up ahead. If he had to guess, a hunter's light with a two hundred yard plus range, mounted to a rifle. His hackles rose. It had to be Wiese. He raced silently forward, then locked his joints and jolted to a stop.

"Well, well. What have we here?"

It was Wiese alright. On his belly, Mateo crept forward. A wolf pup cowered as far from the hunter as he could get. A trap, cruelly clasped around his front paw, gleamed in the dark. Blood spotted the ground around the metal jaws. Mateo's hackles rose. Damn the man. Trapping season for wolves had ended over a week ago. He hated the things on principle and wished they were outlawed, but that wasn't going to happen, at least not in Montana.

Wiese threw the semiautomatic to his shoulder. "You are almost not worth wasting a bullet. Perhaps, I should just club you to death."

Hell. He couldn't very well change out here in the woods and arrest Wiese buck naked. If he'd been on his own property, he had several stashes in the underbrush, but nothing here.

"Yeah, that's exactly what I'm going to do." Wiese brought the gun from his shoulder and holding the barrel with the butt end forward, he approached the whining pup, grinning evilly.

Mateo flew out of the night. His growl fearsome, he knocked Wiese to the ground. Taken by surprise, the poacher dropped the gun. It went off, missing Wiese by inches.

"Jesus Christ," Wiese shrieked, burrowing into the ground.

Mateo grabbed the gun butt awkwardly in his teeth and took off at an ungainly lope. The rifle's sixteen and a quarter inch barrel dragged the ground, catching in holes and grass clumps. A hand gun would have been a hell of a lot easier to carry between his teeth.

"Hey, you come back here with my gun."

Mateo, stretched out his legs, feeling his muscles

uncoil and his stride lengthen, as he raced through the forest, the rifle bumping the ground awkwardly, his head bobbing.

The rifle barrel hit a tree, jerking the stock from his mouth.

Wiese crashed through the underbrush after him.

Hell with it. He kicked debris partially over the gun, covering the green light still streaming from the top of the rifle and waited.

The crashing got louder.

Wiese stomped through the underbrush, holding a hunting knife in front of him.

Mateo growled, his hackles standing straight up.

Wiese stopped. The knife raised. "I want my gun." He looked around. The dark night, undergrowth, and light drizzle kept everything black, except for the occasional flutter of a naked branch that moved like long, ghost-like fingers in the night.

Mateo drew back his lips and snarled a warning.

"I want my gun, you stupid animal."

Mateo's gaze flashed back and forth between the man's taut features and his raised hand. He stood poised, waiting and watching.

The moment Wiese threw the knife Mateo jumped to the right then leaped at Wiese. He fought to control himself, his blood lust running high, the need to bury his fangs in his enemy's gorge strong.

With iron control he held back. He couldn't give in to it neither could he let Wiese get the upper hand.

Wiese fought like a madman, but Mateo had the advantage of knowing what to watch for. They rolled over and over. Time and again, Wiese reached for Mateo, but Mateo always managed to draw back. Instead of biting at the throat as he longed to, he bit at the man's arm padded by his jacket. Wiese managed to get a hit in to Mateo's kidney.

He yelped and bit down harder than he'd intended. "Ouch, you bastard."

Wiese pushed to his feet and began to run. Mateo loped behind him, growling and nipping at his heels.

The poacher stumbled over a tree root and fell.

If he'd been in human form, Mateo would have rolled his eyes. Since he wasn't, he nipped Wiese's leg.

The man kicked out and caught him on the jaw.

Dammit.

Wiese surged to his feet and bolted.

Mateo trailed Wiese to his truck where the poacher jumped in the cab, gunned the engine and took off, throwing gravel everywhere.

Mateo watched the headlights disappear into the night then loped back to the trapped pup.

CHAPTER 6

Awwoooo.

The mournful howl made his skin quiver. He ran faster. As soon as he reached the pup, he changed. The icy drizzle cool against his hot skin.

The pup whimpered, cringing away, much as it had from Wiese.

"Shh now. I'm not going to hurt you. Did you get lost or did Wiese kill your momma? Where's your pack?" He kept his voice soft and low, a musical cadence as he pried open the trap. He pulled the pup out and the trap slammed shut. The noise as sickening as the click of a monster's teeth in the quiet night.

He held the pup in his arms, examining the leg. Wolves never harmed him, considering him dominant. The little one proved it by peeing all over him.

He pushed out a long breath. "Now isn't that just the icing on the cake."

The leg would have to be seen to, plus he couldn't leave the little fellow alone. He'd never survive on his own.

He set him on the ground and watched him limp around on three legs. Whiskers whispered as he scratched his chin. He could run in human form, just not as well nor as long. He sure as hell didn't care for the idea of running buck-ass naked for fifteen miles but he really didn't see where he had a choice. He grabbed up the pup and loped off, wincing as one of his bare feet landed on a protruding rock.

Over an hour later, he arrived at his cabin. The pup clutched in his arms. Wheezing, he stopped to catch his breath.

The stranger in the shadows melted away.

~*~

Strong, stale coffee assaulted Blair's senses. Quinn had made the pot. You could always tell. She backed out, even as Adam saw her and opened his mouth.

The door slammed as she pivoted on her heel and headed across the street to Belle's. A noisy, older red sports car came speeding toward her. The driver laid on his horn and flipped her off.

She turned, stopped and hands on hips gave him an icy stare.

The window came down and a teen with a wispy mustache and pimples stuck his head out, his expression abashed as he screeched to a stop. "Sorry, ma'am, sir, I didn't recognize you."

"That's Chief Deputy Delaney to you, Forrest, and you feel it's okay to run hapless citizens down in the middle of the street as long as they can't arrest you?" She enunciated each syllable giving it a northern bite that still made her brain revolt.

"No sir, er ma'am, er Chief Deputy Delaney." The

flustered youth finally managed to get out.

"You're not going to put me in jail or give me a ticket are you?"

"Oh, Gad, Forrest, don't be an idiot. You didn't shoot anyone. You just were going a few miles over the speed limit in this Godforsaken town, when there wasn't even anyone else on the road." The loud, arrogant voice came from the passenger seat.

She turned her attention to the passenger side and smiled. Or at least showed her teeth. She hadn't had her coffee yet. Putting the fear of God—or the law in this case—into some mouthy little bastard barely past puberty would have to do.

She strode to the passenger side and jerked open the door.

"Now you've done it." Forrest's face turned pasty.

"Out of the car, Jerome."

"Or what?" His voice came out in a high deviant sneer.

"Not a fast learner are you?"

She reached in, grabbed him by the collar and hauled him out.

"Hey, you can't do that."

She tightened the grip on his collar and gave him a shake. "I can't?"

He squawked in response.

Forrest leaned over in the seat. "Ma'am, I mean Chief Deputy Delaney, we're going to be late for school and Mr. Henderson is strict about attendance. It'll mean detention for sure. That's why I was speeding. Not that's any excuse," he added hastily.

"Then you'd better get going, hadn't you?"

"Thank you." His breath whooshed out and relief washed over his face.

He straightened behind the wheel.

"What are you waiting for?"

"Uh, you've still got Jerome."

"He wasn't as smart as you. Now go on before I change my mind."

"Hey you can't do that." A little panic crept into Jerome's defiant posture. He was raised by a hard-working, single mom who worked as a nurse in the small clinic at the edge of town. One doctor. One PA. And four nurses. And Grizzly was lucky to have that.

Blair didn't think it was Mr. Henderson who had Jerome panicked. The principal would contact Jerome's mom, and his mother was no pushover. He might be the town delinquent, but he made straight A's.

"Sorry, man." Forrest drove off at a decorous pace.

Blair coughed as the tail pipe spit black smoke in its wake.

"Listen, I've got to get to school or my mom will skin me."

"I know. How about an apology?"

"For what?" The sneer warred with panic.

"For starters, being an asshole."

A grin flickered in brilliant blue eyes and his lips twitched. He pushed a blond lock off his forehead. He was a good-looking kid when he wasn't practicing being bored and sullen.

"Well I didn't know it was against the law, but I

apologize. I definitely was being an asshole."

Blair knew when to hold and when to fold. "Come on, I'll drive you to school."

They jogged to her SUV. She turned over the engine and turned on the siren and lights, tires screeching as they hit the street.

They pulled in as Forrest got out of his car, his mouth hanging open.

"You're okay, Chief Deputy Delaney." Jerome gave her a male once over, a cheeky grin, threw open the door and loped to the red brick building with double wide doors and floor to ceiling windows beside them.

She shook her head, grinning as she drove back to the station, in a much better mood in spite of caffeine deprivation.

Parking in front of Belle's, she hopped out and tromped inside. A familiar figure with broad shoulders and narrow hips waited at the counter. As if he recognized her tread, he turned, nodded then swiveled back to Belle, a portly woman with a no-nonsense attitude. Delaney liked that in a woman. "Make that two."

Belle gave a brisk nod and set to work.

"I saw the cruiser go racing by with the lights flashing and the siren on."

"I busted young Szoke's ass then drove him to school."

Mateo shook his head. "That kid is either going to be a criminal or a law officer. I haven't figured out which."

"With his mom at the helm, I'm betting on the

police officer." Blair picked up her cup of coffee.

"Good point."

Mateo paid for the coffee and they strolled out.

When they entered the police station, Randy Wiese jumped out of a visitor's chair like there was a spring in the seat.

"Sheriff, you've got to do something."

"About the supposed wolf that attacked your dog? Yeah, we're looking into it." Mateo set down his coffee, took off his jacket and slung it over the spartan steel coat tree beside the door.

"It wasn't the same wolf. This one stole my rifle and sprung my trap."

Mateo leaned casually on the dispatcher's desk and crossed his legs. "And what trap would that be, Randy." While his stance was casual, his eyes were amber chips of ice.

Blair locked her knees to keep from taking an involuntary step back. There was just something about Mateo when his back was up that made anyone with a lick of sense beat a hasty retreat.

"Forget the trap. He stole my gun."

Blair let out an unladylike snort that would have given her poor momma heart palpitations. Yes, her momma still used words like that. "Wiese, have you been drinking again? A wolf takes your gun and springs your trap?"

"No trap. I don't know why I said that. But I'm telling you he took my gun."

"A different wolf took your gun?" Her eyebrows arched high. "Did he try to shoot you with it?"

"Don't be ridiculous. He could drag it, he couldn't aim and fire it."

Smothered snorts were coming from Adam's direction.

Wiese ignored them and plodded on. "It was a different wolf. This one was bigger and had a silver coat, same shade as the gray in the sheriff's hair." He pointed at Mateo.

Now Quinn guffawed. "Something we should know about, Boss?"

"You can laugh all you want, but I know what I saw." Wiese jutted his chin at a stubborn angle.

Only Blair noticed the almost imperceptible stiffening of Mateo's posture when the hair color was mentioned, but she was so entertained by Wiese's story she didn't question it till much later.

"So, what are you going to do, Sheriff?" His nose was small compared to the rest of his face and right now fairly quivering with righteous indignation.

Mateo gazed at Wiese, till the man started to twitch. He took his time before responding. "Go investigate."

"I would think so. It's your job."

Blair shook her head. Randy never knew when to keep his mouth shut.

Mateo took a stride forward that put him right in the complainer's face. "I know what my job is and how to do it."

Wiese held his gaze for a small second before backing off. "Never thought otherwise."

But Mateo's hackles were up. "And if I find so much

as one trap on your land, it'll be confiscated and I'll levy the highest fine on you possible."

"I can guarantee, you'll find no traps."

Thoughtful, Blair tapped her chin. She'd expected defensive posturing, but Wiese looked downright glum. She suspected he set traps offseason. Had someone stolen them? The thought warmed her to the tips of her crimson painted toenails. But if so, who?

"Delaney, let's go."

Mateo broke into her thoughts. He leveled one more look at Wiese then headed for the door.

"I'm coming too. You'll need to know where it took place."

"Of course." Mateo headed for his big SUV and he and Blair climbed in. He turned over the engine. When he noticed Blair turn up her collar and clutch her arms for warmth, he turned up the heat.

Hot air soon blasted out of the vent. Blair gave a shiver of delight.

"I would have thought your blood would have thickened by now. It's been two years since you left Georgia."

"Y'all must have been born with blankets in your veins," she grumbled.

"That's it." He waited for Wiese to pull out then wheeled in behind him.

She'd had the presence of mind to grab their coffee. She placed his in the holder and took a sip of hers then dropped a bomb—at least to her way of thinking. "Jesse Kipp's got a new girlfriend."

CHAPTER 7

"Oh, yeah?" he replied without much interest.

"They say she's a real looker."

He grunted.

She ignored his lack of response. "Apparently, he's completely infatuated. Enough to get permission from the tribe to let him rent her his cabin in the mountains."

That got Mateo's attention. He squirmed in his seat uncomfortably. Once upon a time he and Jesse had been close. The two of them had spent many a weekend at that cabin when they were boys, hunting and fishing. Then he started shape-changing and distanced himself from anyone that might learn his secret. It had left a rift that had never healed. He couldn't blame Jesse for it. If the actions had been reversed, Mateo would have been devastated. They were blood brothers.

He lifted his hand from the steering wheel and glanced at the scar. He'd gotten a little careless when they held the ritual at a bonfire behind the cabin when they were ten and slashed too deep. Jesse's dad had rushed him home. Lucky for Mateo his old man was a medic. He'd stitched him up and admonished him to be more careful in future. Jesse had said it was a visible sign that their bond ran deep. He thrummed the steering wheel with a thumb, uncomfortable with the memory.

The cabin was sacred to Jesse as it had been to his father when he lived there. His father swore that at night he could hear the spirits sing. Jesse wouldn't take just anybody to the cabin unless he was in love or highly infatuated.

"What's she like?"

Blair had just taken a long gulp of coffee, her eyes closed, an expression of caffeinated ecstasy on her features. He stole a quick look. High sharp cheekbones, full lips, a head full of honey-blonde hair and skin like a ripe peach. At least he'd always assumed it would be smooth to the touch. She would age well.

Her eyes opened reluctantly, slowly, like she was just getting out of a tousled bed. "Who?"

He grinned in spite of himself. "Jesse's girl."

"Wasn't that a song?"

"Forget the song, what's she like?"

"How would I know? I've never met her." That full lower lip pushed out, apparently not happy about having her moment interrupted. She frowned. "Though, I've heard rumors. She keeps to herself and the old woman, that a lot of them go to when the doctor isn't around, doesn't like her aura, says she's brought bad medicine to the rez."

A chill ran down his spine. Don't go imagining things, he lectured himself.

"What does the looker look like?"

"Tall, long legs, big breasts, black hair. Or so I've been told."

As she talked an image from his past rose along with his hackles. The wolf started pushing to be free. The need to destroy the evil that had come to his land so strong tamping it down took all his formidable control. It couldn't be her. He'd warned her what would happen if she came back. But if it was... his hands clenched on the steering wheel. What took place before was only the beginning. If not stopped, the attacks would come with more frequency and it wouldn't just be animals that got slaughtered. Her kills and the pleasure in them had escalated before she left.

His head thundered with the need to let his bones change shape.

"Oh yeah, blue eyes."

He sagged and his sweaty palms loosened on the steering wheel. Delilah's eyes were emerald, cold as chips of ice.

He hadn't thought of Delilah Devon in a long time. It disturbed him that he did now. The reason, he'd smelled the evil. And though she'd hid it well till the end, Delilah was evil. The scent of it rotten, coating the crisp clean scent of fresh air and sunshine. Making it hard to breath without gagging.

"So, what do you think about this magical wolf that made off with Randy's gun and the trap? No wait, there was no trap." Her honeyed drawl dripped with sarcasm.

He grinned. He'd tossed the trap. He'd be damned if he let anything else get caught in those cruel jaws. Luckily the pup was going to be okay. He'd tended to its fore leg then left it with the gray wolf. He'd be good company for the old one. Mateo worried about him. He feared when it was his time, he'd crawl off to die before Mateo could say goodbye.

"He's pulling over." Blair broke into his bleak thoughts. Thank the spirits for small favors.

"Yeah." They'd left the two-lane road they'd traveled for a one-lane dirt track a couple of miles ago. They parked close to the spot where Wiese's hound had been slaughtered.

Doors slammed as they got out of the truck.

Wiese waited at the outskirts of the big pines, shifting his feet and cracking his knuckles. "This way." He motioned toward the same trail Mateo'd taken last night. He came to a spot, almost exactly where the hound had been slaughtered. An elusive scent of copper hung in the air and a dried, crusty brown mass coated the grass.

"This is where it happened." Wiese hitched up his pants and pointed at the scuffed up ground. Up ahead he could make out the faint outline of the trap from the broken pine needles but, for the moment, chose to ignore it. The pup must have been frantic with pain and the scent of death around him.

"Did you find the gun?"

Wiese straightened and swelled his chest. "I sure did. The bastard had buried it under some leaves."

"Randy, you're giving me a headache. Wolves don't

heist guns and then bury them." Blair pressed hard at a spot between her eyes.

Mateo bit back a smile. "So, what exactly do you want us to do, Randy?"

"Catch and kill that wolf."

"Which one?"

"Both of them. The black one and the gray."

"And you're sure you saw two different wolves?"

"Yes, I'm sure."

"Alright. We'll work on that."

"Let me know when you get them."

Mateo made a motion with his hand as he walked away.

"If I don't get them first," Wiese called after him.

Mateo stopped, turned. "Today's the fourteenth. Hunting season ends the fifteenth. Don't forget it." He drilled him with a stare that made Wiese wilt.

"Yeah."

"He's nutty as a fruit cake." Blair didn't bother to lower her voice as they tromped through the forest, pine needles cracking under their boots. "He had to be drunk as a skunk. Booze and firearms are a nasty combination."

"You got that right."

They reached the SUV and hopped in.

As Mateo started the truck, Blair asked, "Where to now?"

"The rez."

"Why?"

"I want to meet Jesse's new girlfriend."

CHAPTER 8

Blair blinked. Once. Twice. Then twisted toward him. "Why?"

Mateo turned the wheel right and pushed on the gas. Trees whizzing by changed to open plain, with prairie grass still brown from winter.

He always drove too fast. That was one of the things she liked about him. She drove fast too.

She thrummed her nails—short cut and clean, juxtaposed to her crimson toe nails hidden in sturdy brown boots—on the dashboard waiting for an answer.

When he didn't respond the thrumming got louder.

He glanced at her. She lifted her brows. He turned his attention back on the road.

"How long has she been here?"

Answer a question with a question. Thanks, Mateo. "I don't know. A couple of weeks, maybe."

"And in a span of fourteen days, she gets him to rent out the hunting lodge?"

"So, they hit it off. It happens. You think a woman is involved with this wolf thing?"

"That hunting lodge is sacred to Jesse." He flipped

on his blinker and shot onto the two-lane. "And I'm just eliminating suspects. Opel says it wasn't a wolf that attacked her, though the scratch marks sure look like it."

"Yeah, I guess. How would you know about the hunting lodge?"

"We spent a lot of time together in our misspent youth."

Blair had just started to take a drink of her lukewarm coffee, choked and ended up spitting it onto her leather jacket. "Well shit. Shoot." She wiped the liquid off her jacket.

Mateo threw her a grin. "No point in cleaning up that mouth for me."

"A lady never curses in public, Blair dear." She mimed her mother perfectly. "And my mother's idea of cursing is a couple of well-placed darns or shoots. When she's really upset a crap might escape."

Mateo laughed out loud. As always, the sound sent a shiver of warmth darting through her. She leaned her head back, wishing for the thousandth time she wasn't so obsessed with the sheriff. Wished he was portly, balding and fatherly. Maybe it was a good thing Luke wanted to come out.

She sat straight up. That was it. She'd hadn't been laid since forever. It wasn't Mateo at all just a biological need.

He gave her a quick glance. "What?"

"I need laid." Then closed her eyes and shook her head. What the hell was wrong with her? Where was her damn filter?

"Don't look at me. I don't believe in mixing business and pleasure."

"That's the way to make a girl feel desirable."

"Desire and desirability have nothing to do with it. It's bad policy to get involved with someone you work with."

"Your body is safe with me. I'm in a relationship." She changed the subject from her sex life or lack thereof. "What happened between you and Jesse. I always thought it was a territorial thing. Testosterone and badges."

He shrugged. For a moment sadness flitted across his face then was gone. "We were close then we weren't. It's no big deal."

"Apparently, it is."

"Just drop it okay?"

"Close or not, he's not going to take kindly to you wanting to question his current squeeze. My sources tell me he's besotted."

Mateo shifted in his seat and frowned. "That doesn't sound like Jesse. He's been breaking hearts since seventeen."

"It happens."

"Yeah. It does."

She snorted. "Don't go and tell me you were ever besotted."

"Once." He looked straight ahead, not throwing any glances her way.

"So, what happened?"

"She wasn't as she appeared."

"How so?"

"None of your business, Delaney."

"Are you sure this wasn't just one of your slam and bam girls?"

He heaved out a breath, but said mildly, "Tsk. Tsk. What would your mother say?"

"Probably same as you. Tsk. Tsk."

She leaned back in the seat thinking about what he'd said about his relationship with Jesse. The two positively bristled around each other. What made two best friends, and that's what she was reading between the lines, change so radically toward each other? She could picture the two drawn together as boys. Both loners, quiet-spoken and sharing a love of nature. Whatever had come between them, it must have been a doozy. A girl perhaps? Somehow, she didn't think so. She couldn't imagine a girl coming between a deep friendship. But then what did she know? When passions ran deep, anything could happen. She'd seen enough murders when she was on the Atlanta police force to know that.

Mateo did an abrupt left and cut the motor. She looked around in surprise at the row of double story brick buildings. She'd been so deep in thought she hadn't realized they'd arrived.

As they stepped out of the SUV, the chief of police strode out of the station, the door slamming behind him. The sun hit his black hair giving it indigo highlights. He wasn't as tall as Mateo and a bit more slender. Still she could see why the ladies liked him.

He stopped when he saw Mateo and swung toward the SUV. He nodded at Blair then turned his attention to Mateo. "What do you want, Grey?"

"Hello to you too, Kipp."

Jesse waited.

"Since you asked, I'd like to meet your girlfriend."

For a brief moment, surprise flickered in deep brown eyes, then all expression wiped from his features except cold suspicion. "Why?"

"Just need an itch satisfied."

"Not with her you're not." He bristled.

"Oh, please. You know me better than that."

He snorted then asked, "Why do you want to meet her?"

"There's been some weird things going on in my county. She's new. She might give me a different perspective or she may have seen something."

"She never leaves the rez. So there's no point in you talking to her."

"Then I'm calling in my marker. I want to see her." Mateo straightened, his eyes darkening.

Jesse rose to his full height and took a step forward which brought them toe to toe. "I'll repay your marker, but not now. And don't think about coming on the rez without my permission."

He wheeled and strode down the street.

Mateo leaned against the open truck door and stared after him.

"Well, what now?" Blair asked.

He shrugged. "Nothing. The man doesn't want me on the rez. Probably would have been a waste of time anyway."

Blair swung into the seat, her spidey sense on high

alert. Mateo never gave up this easily. He was planning something and whatever it was, it wasn't good.

~*~

The night air nipped his fur-tipped ears and filled his nostrils with the tangy scent of pine, the luscious smell of rabbit and rich, black loamy earth. He, the old one and the pup frisked about the property enjoying the run and the companionship. It was as close to a pack as he or the old one had ever come. When they reached his property line, the old one sat down on his haunches, his tongue hanging out as he panted. The pup followed Mateo till he turned and growled then the pup raced back to the old one and sat beside him whining. The old wolf licked his ear and the pup subsided.

Mateo lengthened his stride and disappeared into the night, headed for the rez. He wanted to see—and smell—Jesse's new girlfriend for himself. If she had nothing to do with the slaughters and attack on Opel, he'd know and mark her off his suspect list.

Jesse's cabin sprawled twenty miles northwest of Mateo's wooded forty acres.

He loped on, his powerful legs churning the miles. An owl swooped in front of him picking up a hapless mouse in its talons then flew away, its large wings flapping in rhythmic motion.

When he reached the rez, he slowed looking for an uninhabited place to cross. Sniffing the boundary's edge, he trotted on until he reached a barren spot where he could detect no human scent and started across.

A low growl carried on the night wind. Then another and another.

A wolf pack. He had neither the time nor inclination to get into a pissing match with an alpha wolf. He took several slow, cautious steps backward then loped along the border, staying clear of the road and houses.

About a mile down, he found a clear path into the mountains and trotted towards Jesse's cabin.

As he approached the glade, where a small rustic house sat, silence greeted him. There were no night sounds that he remembered from his childhood. Too early in the year for most insects, it should have been alive with night predators and small furry creatures that ventured into the dark.

Then he heard it, a tiny hopeless cry. He shifted and headed toward his left, his paw dislocating a branch.

Clack. A steel-trap snapped around the branch. The sound startling in the quiet.

What the hell? Jesse trapped, but never with steel traps. That was one thing that hadn't changed between the two of them. Both of them hunted, but neither sanctioned the cruel jaws that left an animal in torment.

He heard the cry again and now knew what caused it. He took a branch between his teeth and proceeded with caution, brushing the ground in front of him. Four traps went off before he worked his way to the frightened rabbit, cowering away from the trap as best as it could.

Eek. Eek. Eek.

The scent of warm blood and fear and the frenzied tiny beat of the creature's heart had him fighting the urge to sink his fangs into it. Saliva pooled in his mouth. He shook his large, shaggy head. Not like this. He shifted, a change of bone, a drawing in and found himself kneeling, buck-naked in human form. He sprang the trap and before he could decide what to do with it the animal hopped away on its three good legs. It would survive or it wouldn't, depending on how nature saw fit.

As the bunny disappeared, its white cotton tail visible one moment then gone the next, the blood lust in him dwindled. He switched back to wolf form, picked the branch up in his powerful jaws and continued around the circuit, traps clicking like castanets as he snapped them. A shiver of relief ran through him when he finally cleared a path.

Did Jesse know about the traps? What was the cabin's occupant so afraid of?

It was time to find out. He slunk forward.

The netting wrapped around him, slapping upwards, carrying him high in the air before it settled leaving him trussed like a turkey dangling several feet in the air.

CHAPTER 9

Dammit. This was not good.

He bit at the ropes. He could do it, but it would take him the better part of the night. He cast a wary glance at the cabin, but nothing moved. He neither sensed nor smelled another.

Plop. A drop of blood landed on his paw, his gums bleeding from the constant contact with the coarse hemp. As the rope thinned, he pushed with his front paws.

Ping. One gave way but it wasn't big enough to fit anything but his paw through.

Time to work on another.

His mouth around another small square of rope, he bit at it then stopped, listening. The sound of an engine coming up the mountain grew closer and louder then cut off in front of the cabin. A quiver traveled through his body. He whined. This wasn't the way he'd planned on going out. He lifted his head and sniffed the air.

Shit. Jesse. If he was involved in setting these traps, he was a goner.

Jesse got out of the car and knocked on the door. "Layla?" When there was no answer, he let himself in.

Mateo gnawed frantically, knowing he could be discovered at any moment.

A few minutes later, Jesse came back out.

Good maybe he's leaving. Mateo hung motionless in the air.

Jesse stood with his hands in his pockets. Humming under his breath, he began to meander around the property. A branch cracked under his boot and a trap snapped.

Missed one.

"What the hell?" Jesse pulled a flashlight out of his pocket and followed the periphery of the traps around the property that Mateo had sprung. "Who, put these out here and who sprung them?" he muttered under his breath.

Good question. For a moment, he thought about changing. But only for a moment. Jesse would either think he'd set the traps or was just plain crazy, hanging in a trap buck-naked. Though, that might be better than whoever set them finding him, he reflected glumly.

Light blinded him. The beam shining directly in his eyes. Dammit. If Jesse went to shoot him, he'd have to change.

"Well, what have we here? Wouldn't your pelt make a great addition to my wigwam?"

You don't have a wigwam. Mateo growled.

The moon glinted off a knife that appeared as if by magic in his other hand.

Shit. I'm going to have to change.

The thought had barely formed when the knife

whistled through the air, severing the top rope holding the net. Mateo went tumbling to the ground, his paws flailing.

He jumped to his feet. Jesse stood in front of him, unarmed, his head high, his expression haughty. They stared at each other. The wary wolf. The proud Blackfoot. Slowly Mateo backed up, his hackles on end, afraid he'd step in another trap.

When he felt it was safe, he turned and ran.

"I know who you are." The words pitched to carry on the quiet night.

~*~

She'd just shucked her clothes and crawled into bed for some much-needed rest when the phone rang.

Grumbling, she reached for the cell. "Chief Deputy Delaney." And lay back against the pillow.

"Blair." Leroy the night dispatcher's voice crackled with urgency.

"What's wrong?" She shot up in bed.

"It's Rose."

"What about Rose?" Her stomach clenched and she ran her free hand through her hair.

"She's been attacked. She's in the hospital."

"What happened?"

"I don't know. The details are sketchy at best. She's asking for you and the sheriff."

"Have you called the sheriff?" She tucked the phone under her ear and pulled on her pants.

"Can't reach him."

She cursed under her breath. Why didn't the man

get a cell, instead of relying on the radio in his car and home? He needed to be available twenty-four seven. The rest of them were. "I'll swing by and pick him up then head for the hospital." She clicked off.

The digital clock glowed three a.m. Probably shacked up somewhere. Still it was odd. Mateo was the most responsible man she knew, except for his phone. Tossing on the rest of her clothes, she finger-combed her hair then trotted to the SUV. Shoving it in reverse, she spun down the drive and into the lane where she threw it in gear and sped toward Grey's.

Fear had her driving faster than she should.

Rounding a sharp curve, she threw on her breaks, making them scream.

A six-pronged buck stood in the middle of the road.

As her car spun from side to side, the buck leaped into the air, his back hooves hitting the back-side door and disappeared into darkness.

"Damn all nocturnal creatures everywhere." Hunched over the wheel she finally got it straightened out and dropped her speed to just a few miles over the speed limit.

She continued to vent with every curse word she'd learned at police academy and a few more. By the time she pulled into Mateo's long drive, she'd calmed down.

"Dammit." Again she had to throw on her brakes as the old wolf, who lurked around Mateo's, loped across the lane after a wolf pup with a bandaged front paw. She hit the horn for good measure. The sound shrill and irritating in the quiet of the night. The pup sped up, the old wolf threw her a look of disdain.

"What is it with animals running out in the road tonight?"

She hopped out of the car, her heels clumping as she ran across the porch, and pounded on the door. "Mateo, are you there?"

She pounded again. No response.

Letting out the air stuck in her belly, she plopped down on the porch and thrummed her fingers on the wood planks. What the hell had happened to Rose?

.~*~

Mateo loped toward the house, every muscle in his body aching. The refrain, "I know who you are," echoing in his head.

Could Jesse possibly know? And if so, why hadn't he confronted him before now?

The old wolf slunk out of the shadows. The pup yipped, cavorting around him, holding his hurt paw up as he danced around on three.

The old wolf paced with him till they neared the house then he plopped down in the shadows. He looked from the old wolf to the house where the porch light shone through the darkness like a beacon and approached.

He stopped in the shadows of the pines. Close enough to see Blair but deep enough into the gloom to blend.

Something was wrong, her whole posture shouted despair. Still he took a moment to drink her in, as he always did when she wasn't aware. She drew him, inexplicably like a finely forged steel link that bound him to her. It wasn't the fact that they worked together that made him keep her at arm's length but the fact that if he got any closer, he couldn't keep his secret from her.

His eyes heated and his heart galloped, the desire to mate always strong when in wolf form. For the most part he kept her at bay, but at night in his dreams she strode in, not stealthily but with an arrogant toss of her head, hair spinning like spun gold onto her shoulders, muscled legs taut, arms smooth and strong, breasts firm.

But right now, he just wanted to scoop her up and console her, something else he dare not do.

He shook himself, loped to the back of the house, his paws crushing the earth and filling his nostrils with the familiar scent of pine and loam as he changed from wolf to man. He let himself in the back door and silent as a wraith threw on his pants and shirt without bothering to button it.

On silent feet, he padded through the house and threw open the door.

"Blair?"

"Chrissake, Mateo, you aged me ten years." She jumped up clutching her heart.

"Where did you come from? You weren't in the house." She looked wildly around.

"I was in the woods. I came in through the back. What's up?"

"You are one spooky dude."

He waited.

Her breath caught and her expression changed. "It's Rose."

"What about Rose?" A premonition had his hackles rising and his gut clenching.

"She was attacked."

His jaw hardened. He knew it. Knew it before Blair said anything.

"Is she okay?"

"I don't know. She's in the hospital."

Grizzly's hospital was more of a clinic with a handful of hospital beds.

"Let's go."

He was striding off the porch before she could stop him. "Grey."

"Yeah?" He kept going.

"You need to get some boots on."

"Right." He glanced down at his bare feet. It just went to show how shaken he was.

"I'll be right back." He trotted into the house, tossed on his boots, grabbed his jacket and gun and ran out. Blair was already in the passenger side of the SUV, engine running.

Mateo got to the outskirts of Grizzly in less than ten minutes and through it in less than that.

"You drive like a maniac. You nearly took out that stray cat." Blair's nails curved into the dashboard.

"I was nowhere near that cat."

"So, you say."

"So, you say? What are we in kindergarten?"

Blair lapsed into affronted silence.

Mateo took a sharp turn into the clinic lot, pulled

into a No Parking space near the front of the clinic and turned off the engine.

Throwing open the door, he hopped out and headed towards the double glass doors, where welcoming light poured out. Blair slid out and in three quick strides caught up. They marched through the doors together and headed for the back of the building where the small ward was located.

The click of their heels echoed in the quiet, dim lit, white-walled hall. A portly nurse, stepped out of a room on their left. She jerked in surprise then straightened rounded shoulders and walked toward them. "Sheriff, Chief Deputy."

The sheriff gave a clipped nod of his chin.

"Hi, Pearl. How is she?" Blair hooked her thumbs in the front pockets of her jeans.

"Weak. Tired. And though she won't admit it, a little scared."

"How did she get here?" Mateo asked.

"Drove herself. Lost a lot of blood in the process."

"What exactly happened?"

"She's not saying." Pearl shook her head causing her iron-gray curls to bounce.

"What's your best guess?"

She hesitated then looked Mateo in the eye. "She has bite and scratch marks on her back and shoulders and the side of her neck. That one was deep. Her face and hands are scraped as if she landed face down in rocks and bracken. I'd say an animal except there's a spot on the side of her head as if she were hit by a rock."

"Maybe, she fell and hit her head," Blair said.

"Maybe." Pearl motioned them through the door and closed it behind them.

Rose lay in bed, her round face pasty and scratched, bandages on the side of her head and neck as white as her face. The cheery yellow room a sharp contrast to the patient.

Blair rushed forward. "Oh, Rose, what happened?" She gently clasped the woman's hand.

"Rose." Mateo stepped forward, anger churning deep in his belly. She was one of his. Whoever had done this would regret it.

"Boss."

"Tell us what happened." His face gave nothing away, his tempestuous emotions in check.

She shook her head. "I don't know if I can." A shudder rippled along her body.

He put a comforting hand on her shoulder. "It's okay, Rose. You're safe. Just start at the beginning."

She took a deep, quavery breath and began, "Mrs. Donaldson's cat got out of the house again."

They were familiar with Mrs. Donaldson's cat. The yellow tom looked as tottery and insubstantial as his owner. Mrs. Donaldson was ninety-one and her vision and hearing were about gone. She'd once let a raccoon in the house that she'd mistaken for her feline.

"And this couldn't have waited till morning?" Mateo kept his voice even and didn't howl as he longed to.

"You know how she is, boss. The poor thing is terrified coyotes will get Mr. Timms."

"Mr. Timms is too stringy for even coyotes to gnaw on. I'm assuming she didn't call the station but called you directly."

Rose nodded.

"Doesn't everyone?" Blair put in. "You need to start fielding your calls and making them go through the station. You don't need to be chasing a kitty cat in the dead of night in a sparsely populated area."

"I'm sure you would have turned her down if she'd called you."

"In a New York minute."

"We aren't in New York or Atlanta and you know you would have done the same."

The indignant color in Rose's round cheeks pleased Mateo. Better that she be irritated with Blair than frightened.

"So, what happened next?"

"I heard a cat crying and followed the sound till I was away from the house." Her words slowed and she started plucking at the white blanket that covered her to her waist. "A figure came out of the dark, dressed in black, wearing a hoodie under a black leather jacket."

"Male? Female?" Mateo asked. His pulse picking up, his senses alert.

Again, she shook her head. "I just don't know. Whoever, whatever, it was tall and slender. Not as tall as you, more about Blair's height. Maybe an inch or so taller. About five ten, I'd say. Whoever, whatever held a rock. Before I could disarm it, it lobbed the rock and knocked me to the ground." She pointed to the bandage on the side of her head.

Holding her hand, Blair asked, "Why do you keep saying it?"

"You're going to think I'm a crazy old woman."

"Never." Blair gently pushed tendrils of damp hair from Rose's face. "And you are certainly not old."

Rose gave a trembly smile. Her ample bosom heaved as she expelled air. She continued to pluck at the blanket and her voice dropped. "Before I could get up, it was on my back, biting at my neck and shoulders, clawing me. It wasn't human. It growled and slobbered on me like a dog. You don't need to tell me it's not possible. I know it."

"How did you get away?" Mateo drummed his fingers against his thighs.

Rose gave a watery chuckle. "Mr. Timms came running out of the underbrush shrieking for all he was worth, his hair standing on end. It startled my attacker. It gave one last lick along the back of my neck." She shuddered. "Then it was gone. I rolled over in time to see someone running away. A human. In those black jeans and black hoodie. He, it, disappeared into the night before I could even get to my feet. Mr. Timms shot out after it, then sat down, wiped his face and trotted toward home. That cat saved my life."

Delilah is afraid of cats.

The thought rose unbidden.

She's back. Has to be. And somehow, she's learned how to control her shifting.

He rubbed at the growing pressure between his eyes.

"I'm going through menopause. Maybe it's causing

me to see things."

"You're not crazy and you're not seeing things. Opel's story was similar. Except for the licking and biting." Blair grimaced. "There's a logical explanation for what's going on. We just have to figure out what it is."

Mateo bit back a grin. Except for her spidey sense, Blair was very much the pragmatist.

"Do you think it's a zombie?" Rose leaned forward and whispered.

Not so much Rose.

"There are no such things as zombies," Blair said firmly. "Now you get some rest. The sheriff and I will figure this out."

Rose nodded, leaned back against the pillows and closed her eyes. Deep shadows circled them.

They let themselves out of the room and tromped down the hall, their boots echoing in the quiet. Blair blasted through the double doors. The night air chill and refreshing after the warm stale air of the clinic.

"I don't know who is doing this, but when I find him, I'm going to kick his ass." She yanked open the SUV's passenger door and slammed it shut behind her.

Mateo jogged over and got behind the wheel. "Get in line."

Blair unwrapped a piece of gum and popped it in her mouth as he backed up the SUV, threw it in first and wheeled out of the parking lot. "So, what do you make of that?" Her gum crackled.

He grunted.

"You don't believe in that zombie crap do you?"

"No. I don't believe in zombies." Shifters but not zombies.

"It's got to be some crazy, getting their rocks off by dressing up like an animal. You know canine teeth, that sort of thing."

"Maybe." He drove sedately through town then opened it up once they were on the deserted highway.

"What else could it be?" She popped her gum loud enough to make him wince.

"That's what I intend to find out. Listen, I want you to do me a favor."

CHAPTER 10

"Some favor," Blair groused to herself as she leaned over the wheel of her SUV and headed toward the reservation.

How in sweet hell was she supposed to get a picture of Jesse's girlfriend and why did Mateo want it?

When she'd balked he'd changed the favor to a command. All he'd say, the woman was a stranger that had arrived about the time the attacks started.

Eyes on the road, she opened the window then fumbled for her coffee. Fresh air nipped her face and swirled her hair. It was going to be one of those days that confirmed her decision to move to Montana. The sun crested the earth in a ball of gold glory, making her squint. The mountains shimmered a hazy bluish-green in the distance and the sky went from pinky-gray to a clear crystal blue. Green sprouts interspersed with shriveled brown grass as far as the eye could see.

It would probably snow tomorrow, but hey, why borrow trouble.

She took a sip of the expresso she'd picked up on the way out and hummed off tune as she rolled down the road.

The clock on her dash showed 6:59 a.m. as she parked in front of Wanda's Coffee Shack. Jesse usually breakfasted there before heading for the police station. She hopped out of her cruiser, clomped across the sidewalk and shoved through the door. Stopping in the entryway, she looked around for Jesse. Her stomach rumbled at the combined scents of bacon, eggs and coffee.

Jesse sat at a booth in the back, facing the door. Smart. He could see anyone coming and going. He raised a hand in greeting then motioned her back. She nodded and swung in his direction. He and Mateo might have problems but she and Jesse were pals. A head of shiny blue-black hair gleamed from the other side of the booth. Maybe she going to meet the illusive girlfriend at last.

She stopped in front of the booth and blinked. Holy Moly.

"So, what brings you to Browning, Chief Deputy Delaney?" Jesse smiled at her.

Her lips went up in response. The Chief of Police didn't smile often but when he did, it lit up his whole face.

"You, breakfast and information. Almost in that order."

A laugh rumbled in his throat and he scooted over. "Sit. Eat."

"Thanks."

Once she'd settled in, he flung up a hand in the direction of his breakfast companion. "This is my friend, Layla Sosa."

"Chief Deputy." She held out her hand.

Blair clasped it. A tingle of electricity ran from her fingertips to her toes, making her eyes widen and her breath catch. She yanked her hand back. The woman across from her was one of the most beautiful Blair had ever seen. Ebony hair and eyes so blue they looked black, with a creamy white complexion. Tacked on to that, screaming sexuality. She even gave off a musky scent of earth and animal. Blair, who considered herself a lusty heterosexual, fought against a lightning attraction. One she didn't care for, not one little bit.

Layla gave her a mocking smile. She knew her affect. Blair couldn't help thinking that Jesse's girlfriend didn't limit herself to men. "Nice to meet you, Miss Sosa." She gave her a cool nod.

"Call me, Layla."

"Layla."

A young man came loping out of the kitchen with a white towel wrapped around his waist. "Hey, Blair. What can I get you?"

"Hi, Tom." She jerked her head toward Jesse's plate. "I'll have what the Chief is having."

"You got it."

"You seem pretty familiar here." Layla leaned in, still wearing that mocking smile.

"Oh, yeah, Wanda serves the best breakfast in the area."

"Don't let Belle hear you say that." Jesse laughed.

She shuddered dramatically. "The last person I want to offend is Belle. Excuse me, I think a text is coming in." She pulled her phone out of her pocket and angled it away from Jesse and snapped a quick pic of Layla before pretending to scroll up and down, her nose pressed against the screen. Then snapped the phone off and shoved it in her pocket.

"Anything important?" Layla asked, her eyes narrowed.

"Nothing that can't wait." She made a dismissing gesture with her hand and gave Layla a bright smile.

Tom came loping back and placed a plain white mug filled with steaming black coffee in front of her.

"Thanks, Tom." She flashed a smile.

He flushed, nodded, then wheeled toward the kitchen.

"The kid's got a crush on you. And Layla," he added, giving his girlfriend a besotted smile. Layla reached over and ran a blood-red fingernail along the back of his hand. "You think everyone has a crush on me."

"Only because it's true. It's a good thing you don't leave the cabin much or the whole populace of Browning would be in an uproar."

"You like your privacy?" Blair turned her attention to the siren.

"Don't you?" Layla purred.

Blair shrugged, fighting the woman's mesmerizing gaze. "I'm a city girl. I'm used to people and crowds."

"Hmm. So, you work for Mateo?" Layla sipped her coffee, eyeing Blair over the rim of her mug.

"You know Mateo?" Blair's spidey sense began to

tingle.

"Everyone's heard of Mateo."

At least, all the sluts.

Jesse cut into the uncomfortable undercurrent, whether intentionally or unintentionally Blair had no way of knowing. Or maybe he was just getting the conversation off Mateo. "So, what can I do for you, Blair?"

"We had another incident last night." She spoke to Jesse but kept her gaze on Layla. The woman's expression turned sly and she showed her teeth in what almost passed for a smile. The hair on the back of Blair's neck rose. For a moment she'd seen something pure animal lurking in the beautiful woman's eyes. Mateo might be on the right track with this one after all. She shook her head. No, it wasn't possible.

"And?" Jesse prodded.

"I know he asked once before, but he was wondering if you'd remembered any new faces on the reservation." Her gaze slid to Layla's where it caught and held.

"So, of course, he thinks anyone causing trouble is Native American." Jesse sneered.

She fought off the force of Layla's stare and turned to Jesse. "You know, where the law is concerned, Mateo is color-blind."

"I'll give the bastard that one."

"What happened to you two? Mateo said you used to be friends."

His head jerked up in surprise. "He told you that?"

"Yes, were you?"

He gave a harsh cold laugh, his dark eyes flat. "Blood brothers. No two young men were closer."

"What happened?"

"You'll have to ask him. Here comes your breakfast." His voice hearty, as if glad of the distraction. The tension in her shoulders relaxed, both of them happy for a change in subject. The only one unaffected, Layla who wore a sphinx smile.

One thing Blair was certain of. She might be attracted to the woman in a very unhealthy way, but she certainly didn't like her.

She turned her attention to the plate in front of her. The aroma making her mouth water. She placed her hand on her stomach to keep it from growling. "Thanks, Tom." She lifted a fork and dug in.

"We may have a small handful of new inhabitants. I'll run a list when I get back to the office and fax it to you."

"Thanks, Jesse," she said around a mouthful of cheesy scrambled eggs.

"No problem. You just tell your boss, he's not welcome on the reservation, in any form, unless he clears it with me first."

Swallowing her eggs, she raised her cup and paused before bringing it to her lips. In any form? She gave a mental shrug and slurped her coffee. Just a figure of speech.

She bolted down her breakfast, threw money on the table and stood.

Layla rose too. "I have to use the little girls' room."

Somehow or other they bumped into each other as Blair headed for the door and Layla the restroom. Blair jumped back. Layla smiled knowingly.

Delaney had her game face on but the hussy unnerved her. She gave a curt nod and made herself stride toward the door, not bolt. Once through it, she picked up speed, jumped in her SUV and raced out of town, blasting the radio on the ride back. By the time she pulled into her parking spot across the street from the station, she'd calmed down.

Trotting across the street, she reached for the door then took a hasty step back as Quinn came bolting through it.

"Quinn?"

"I'm heading for the hospital." He didn't slow down—just kept moving like a steam roller on steroids.

"Any changes? Is she okay?" she called after him.

"She damn well better be," floated back as he headed down the alley to his pickup parked around back.

"Any word on Rose?" she asked Adam as she crossed the office threshold.

"Sheriff called a little while ago. She's okay. He just broke the news to me and Quinn. Looks like I'm dispatching today."

"I'm surprised Leroy didn't tell you."

"His wife had a flat tire while driving and landed in a ditch. He was a bit preoccupied when he left."

"Is she okay?"

"Yeah, she's fine. Just a little shook."

Mateo stuck his head out. "Any luck?"

"Did you doubt it?" She bragged then reached in her pocket. Her breath caught square in her chest and pressure built between her eyes. "That bitch stole my phone."

CHAPTER 11

Blair wheeled on her heel and headed toward the door.

What the hell?

"Delaney, in my office." Mateo spoke with what he considered commendable calm considering that if Blair had proof, she didn't any longer.

Adam's head swiveled back and forth between them, a look of confusion on his young face.

Blair stomped into the office and dropped into the hard-backed chair in front of his scarred, wooden desk. He pushed aside a stack of papers and propped himself against it then crossed his legs.

"I take it you met Jesse's current squeeze?"

"Squeeze is exactly what she is. I've never met anyone in my life that gives off so much sexuality. Your fine self included."

He threw her a startled look. She sat thrumming her fingernails on the edge of the desk. She had a mad going alright. So much so she hadn't even realized what she'd said. And a good thing too.

"I take it you met her."

"Sure did. Had breakfast with her and Jesse. I got a picture of her while claiming to check a text."

"What was she like?"

"I told you. She's a sensual creature. Most beautiful woman I've ever met. No wonder Jesse is infatuated. She was giving me ideas for a red-hot minute and I don't do women."

Mateo blinked. Delaney affected by a woman? He stiffened. It had to be Delilah. "What did she look like?"

"I told you. Beautiful."

"Chief Deputy. Give me a description."

Blair settled. "Black hair, like I told you before. Blue eyes. Tall. I'm five nine. I'd say she's five ten. Slender. Muscled. No identifying marks."

If it wasn't for the eyes, it fit Delilah's description to a T. He jerked upright and nearly slapped himself in the head. Contacts.

"You're right." Blair leaned forward in her seat.

"About what?"

"She's definitely involved in this." She shot out of her chair. "That means she hurt Rose. I'm going on to the rez and haul her sorry ass back here."

"Blair, sit down."

She stood undecided.

"Sit."

She plopped down.

"Why do you think it's her? Your spidey sense?"

"Don't diss the spidey sense." Then scrunched her face, shook her head and shrugged her shoulders as she explained. "Her eyes gleamed when the incidents were mentioned. Like she was laughing up her sleeve."

A knock sounded at the door.

"Come in."

Adam opened it and handed Blair her phone.

She gaped. "Where did you get it?"

"Jesse just dropped it off. Said he found it on the sidewalk outside the café."

"Thanks, Adam." She reached for it.

Adam plopped it in her hand then left, closing the door.

"Picture's going to be gone," Mateo said.

She punched eagerly at the phone. Then her face fell. "Damn her."

"How'd she get it?"

"She bumped into me as I was leaving." She scowled. "Don't say a word."

Oldest trick in the book. He manfully restrained from making the comment and threw up his hands in mock surrender.

"What now?" She brought the chair she'd been balancing on two legs to the floor.

"Why don't you see if Tina could give us a composite?"

Scarlatina was a local artist in the area. They called her in whenever they needed a drawing. A full-blooded Blackfoot, she lived off the rez and occasionally did composites for both he and Kipp.

"Will do." She sprang out of her chair and bolted for the door.

He winced as it slammed shut behind her. Blair only knew one speed and that was full throttle. He shuffled the papers on his desk. Funny how he and Jesse had both ended up in law enforcement. Then again maybe not. His dad had always called them different sides of the same coin. If Delilah or whoever she was calling herself these days had hooked up with Jesse, it was going to make a complicated situation worse. His former best friend wouldn't believe a word that came out of his mouth.

~*~

Blair stepped out of her SUV and took a deep appreciative breath of ponderosa pine. Tina's rangy house had woods on the west side and back. The front and east side of the house was open field. The east side, made completely of glass, housed her studio.

She strode to the porch and knocked on the door.

No answer.

She knocked again.

Still no answer.

With a sigh, she pushed open the door and yelled, "Tina, are you home?"

A moment later a slender young woman, several inches shorter than Blair with black hair shoved into a messy bun, came walking out wiping her hands on a paint-stained rag and embraced her. "Hey, Blair."

Blair returned the hug then let go. "How many times have I told you to lock your door?"

Tina laughed. "This makes a hundred and one."

Blair grumbled. "It's not funny. I could have been a rapist or a murderer."

"But you're not." She gave Blair's arm a light rub.

"Could have been."

"Did you come all the way out here to yell at me?"

Tina grinned at Blair, her head tipped.

"I need a composite."

"Sure, no problem. Come into the studio."

Blair followed her friend. Tina was a hermit when she painted, but when she came up for air, she and Blair would let off steam over a few brews. They'd go to Browning, East Glacier or Grizzly.

As they entered the studio, Blair cast an appreciative look out the glass wall where feeders were placed for the wildlife. A mockingbird, on a blue feeder, grumbled at a red squirrel. Juncos and chickadees threw husks from used seeds on the ground while industrious sparrows hopped at the bottom of the feeder looking for food.

An easel sat in the center of the room with a half-finished buffalo herd racing across the prairie.

Tina strode to her desk and pulled out a tablet and charcoal pencil.

Blair plopped down in a nearby chair and begin to talk. As she described Layla, Tina's pencil flew. Blair finished her description. Tina made a few more strokes then looked up. A frown flitted across her features. "This sounds like the sheriff's new girlfriend."

Blair nearly bounced in her chair. She leaned forward, her breathing quick and light. "That's exactly who it is."

"Why do you want a picture of Layla?"

"I don't. Mateo does and you know his history with Jesse."

"Why not just take a phone shot? Jesse has no

problem with you."

"Been there done that. Bitch managed to steal my phone. When I got it back, the picture had been deleted."

"Interesting." Tina made a few more strokes, used an eraser than drew again. Finished, she handed the pad to Blair.

Blair's breath caught. "How did you manage to catch her essence?" A chill crawled along her spine. The woman on the paper emitted sultry beauty—and evil.

Instead of answering, Tina asked, "What's this about?" Her chair squeaked as she leaned back into worn brown leather, with a scratch on the side of the seat.

"You heard about the attack on Opel Caulfield, right?" She didn't mention Rose. Couldn't. Or she'd get pissed all over again.

Tina's head shot up. "Someone attacked Opel?"

"Where have you been?"

Tina pointed at the easel.

"Gotcha. Attacked Opel, killed their prize bull, and Randy Wiese's hunting hound. Randy claims a wolf killed his hound and took off with his hunting rifle." Blair couldn't help it. She bent over laughing, letting out a couple of unladylike snorts.

Tina grinned from ear to ear. "That certainly sounds like a wolfie thing to do." They both chortled. She shook her head. "He needs to leave the hard stuff alone."

Blair rose and stretched, feeling better than she

had all day. She tore the drawing from the tablet. "Thanks for this. I'll give it to the sheriff. Just send us the bill."

"Want a latte for the road?"

Blair flashed a grin at her friend. "Does a wild bear sh—er do his business in the forest?"

"Unless he has a contract for a toilet paper commercial."

That set them off again.

Bent over, Blair held up a hand. "Stop. You're killing me."

Tina patted her on the back and headed for the kitchen where she pulled a to-go cup out of the cabinet, filled it with coffee, chocolate syrup and creamer, poured it over ice then handed it to Blair. "There ya go. My painting should be finished in a few days. Ready for a girl's night out?"

"You bet. Call me."

"Will do." Blair left, cold caffeine in hand and the drawing of Jesse's girlfriend in her jacket pocket. She couldn't wait to see the sheriff's face when he looked at the sketch. Something more was going on than he let on. She'd bet her next cup of java on it.

She hopped in the SUV, tunes blasting, sipping her latte, anxious to see Mateo's reaction to the drawing. It was a half hour drive from Tina's place to Grizzly. She made it in twenty.

Someone had taken her parking spot, which had her cursing. It wasn't actually reserved but everyone in town knew she parked there. She managed to squeeze into a spot made for a smaller vehicle without bumping or scratching the car in front or behind.

Pleased with herself, she strutted into the office. A decent latte and seeing her bestie always put her in a good mood. Not to mention her parking feat.

"Uh, Blair." Adam tried to wave her down while handling the phone and dispatch at the same time.

"Be right back. Just got to give Mateo something."

"But Blair—"

She tapped on the door and without waiting for permission strolled in and tossed the drawing on his desk.

The sheriff could hide his emotions better than anyone she knew, but he couldn't control the blood that drained from his face or the musky animal scent he gave off as he stared at the drawing. Her skin began to prick. "Do you know her?"

He didn't respond, just continued to stare at the drawing.

"Mateo, do you know her?"

He didn't answer just pointed toward the far wall with his index finger.

"What?"

Drumming his fingers on the desk, he didn't bother to answer.

From behind her a throat cleared.

She whirled. Her breath caught and her jaw dropped. "Luke?"

CHAPTER 12

"Hey, Delaney."

A man in black jeans, a maroon Henley, and a black leather jacket pushed away from the dull grayish-green wall he leaned on. He had blonde hair and screamed city boy.

He strode to her, yanked her into his arms and planted a hot, wet one on her. A kiss of possession. She writhed in embarrassment.

When her boss cleared his throat, she pushed Luke away, hard enough to make him stagger.

"This isn't exactly, the welcome I was expecting." He flashed her a grin. One that two years ago would have made her knees weak.

"What are you doing here?" She stepped out of grabbing range.

"I had a few days leave coming and thought I'd surprise you."

"You did that alright." Then forced a smile on her stiff, hot face. "Listen, I've still got several hours to work." She dug in her pockets for her keys.

Before she could toss them, Mateo said, "Take the rest of the afternoon off, Delaney. You've put in more than your share of overtime."

She looked him in the eye, forcing down the heat that still tried to rise up her olive-colored collar. If he sneered or laughed, she'd bean him, even if he was her boss.

His face was devoid of all feeling. Suddenly, she remembered the drawing. She pointed at it. "Did you recognize her?"

His face, if anything, went blanker. Something she would not have thought possible. "Later. Get on out before I change my mind."

She started to argue, to push for a response, before her sense of self-preservation kicked in. "Okay. See you tomorrow. Call me if you need me."

He gave a short nod.

As they walked out, his hand on her back, Luke dipped his head in acknowledgement. "Sheriff."

"Detective."

Neither man smiled.

When she got to Adam, she stopped. "What did you want to tell me?"

He grinned and pointed his chin at Luke. "That you've got company."

"Any news on Rose?"

"She's better. She'll be going home tomorrow."

"Great. Does she need a ride?"

This time his grin was filled with mischief. "Quinn's driving her home. He'll be in after he gets her squared away."

She laughed and winked at him.

As they strode out and headed for the SUV, she said, "You should have let me know you were coming.

There's no groceries in the house except coffee and granola bars."

"What difference would it have made? You can't cook." He laughed and reached for her hand.

She pulled it back. "Chief deputies don't hold hands, especially in Grizzly." She nudged him in the ribs. "I can't cook but you can."

"Same old Delaney. And here I was afraid you might have changed." He headed left.

She grabbed his arm. "I'm parked over there."

"And I'm parked here." He pointed at a sleek red sports car.

"Nice. How did I miss that? Rental?"

"Yeah."

"You flew in to Glacier?"

"That's right."

"I'll meet you at the house."

"You still in that cabin in the sticks?"

"That's right. Got a problem with it?"

He gave her a slow once over. "All that privacy? Not hardly."

Heat surged through her. Real sex. It'd been awhile.

"I'll meet you there. Not that you'll beat me, but if you do, the key is under the red flowerpot with the wilted plant in it."

"Come on, Delaney. You're a cop. You can do better than that." He fisted his hands on his hips.

"Around here it's high security." She flashed him a grin and bolted to her car.

Her SUV had power but once outside of town he

flew around her like she was standing still. "I should give you a ticket," she yelled at the disappearing taillights.

When she got to her cabin, he was nowhere in sight, his car parked in the drive. She put her hand on the hood. Still warm. He hadn't beaten her by much. She ran up the steps and threw open the door. His eyes gleaming, he stood waiting.

"Why do you still have your clothes on?" She grabbed his coat and yanked it off. He did the same. In less than a minute they were stripped down and she was up against the wall. The sex hot, intense and fast. Her legs still around him, she mumbled into his shoulder. "I've missed this."

"I've missed you." He kissed the top of her head. "Want to try it again in the bedroom at a pace that won't kill me."

"Works for me."

Blair wrapped around him, he weaved into the bedroom, his breath coming in gasps. "Out of shape."

"Could have fooled me."

An hour or so later, they lay spent, sprawled on the bed.

She noticed his glance around her stark white-walled room. He gave a pleased huff at the bedside table lamp with a ceramic star on the black base he'd given her for Christmas last year. Then his gaze switched to a picture of them in the islands where they'd taken a getaway vacay, right before she moved out here. Truth beknown, she was surprised they were still together. Two years had to be a record for a long-distance relationship.

"I don't think your boss likes me much." He stretched then nuzzled her neck.

"Oh, that's just Mateo. He's not a warm and fuzzy guy."

"Truth is I don't like him much either."

"What the hell is that about?"

She sat up in bed, letting the sheet fall to her waist.

He gazed at her appreciatively and reached for her. She placed his hand back on the bed. "What's your problem with Mateo?"

"My problem is, I think you like him too much."

"Where is this coming from?" She pushed the hair back from her face, got out of bed and threw on a set of sweats.

He leaned up again the bed board.

She studied him. Luke had outstanding pecs.

"Maybe I'm jealous that I'm on the other side of the country and you're working for a hot sheriff."

"You think Mateo is hot?"

"Don't you?"

She shrugged. "I've never noticed."

"You're lying, Delaney. You always notice."

"You've got nothing to worry about." She dug around the dresser till she found a scrunchie and pulled her hair into a tail.

"Aren't you getting tired of phone sex?"

She ran a light nail along his chest. "Well it's sure not as good as this."

He grabbed her hand. "We've been together for three years."

"Yeah, and what's your point?" She tugged it loose and bent to pull on some worn white tennies next to the bed.

He rolled on his side and propped his head up with his hand. "We've never really talked about getting married."

Christ Jesus. "I'm in Grizzly, Montana and you're in Atlanta, Georgia, remember?" She wiped her sweating palms.

"I've been offered a job with the Billings police department."

"What?" She whipped around.

"I'm asking you to marry me, Blair." He shrugged. "Guess I should have waited for a more romantic setting."

She wiped her palms again. The suckers wouldn't stop sweating. "Listen, Luke, marriage isn't my thing."

"We could try living together."

"I don't know. I just don't know." She got up and paced the room, bumping into the dresser in the process.

Bed springs groaned as he pushed off the bed and headed for the door. She assumed to retrieve his pants. He stopped in the doorway and turned. "Just think about it okay?"

"Yeah. Sure."

When he disappeared down the narrow little hall, she dropped her head in her hands and groaned. What the hell was she supposed to do about this latest development?

~*~

Mateo tossed back his third cup of coffee of the morning as he sat at his desk staring at the drawing, now smudged from handling. Between thoughts of Delaney in bed with Hanigan and certainty about who was behind the attacks, he hadn't had the most restful night's sleep. A headache thrummed in the back of his head from keeping the wolf—who longed to burst out snarling and snapping—at bay.

Delilah Devon, author of his most erotic fantasies and darkest nightmares. He'd been besotted by her, possibly spelled, till he'd seen her murky side. She was evil. Pure and simple. She enjoyed inflicting pain and fear. When he finally burst through the sexual haze she'd wove around him and started thinking with his head instead of his man parts, he ordered her to leave and never come back.

It hadn't been pretty. She told him before it was over she'd have him on his knees begging and doing other things as well. That was four years ago. The first year he'd spent looking over his shoulder, always on the alert for her. But when she didn't return, he'd decided she'd moved on. Hoped to hell she had. Wrong again.

He rubbed the back of his head where the pounding was the strongest.

What to do now? There was no use trying to explain to Jesse, even if he'd talk to him which was unlikely. Kipp was in the infatuation stage just as he'd once been. The only thing he'd get for his trouble was a pop on the nose. And if memory served, the chief of police had a pretty strong right.

No, he'd just have to patrol at night. Maybe have Delaney do some patrolling too. He rejected the idea nearly as soon as he had it. He had no doubt it was Delilah who'd hurt Rose—he wasn't about to give her a shot at Delaney. Just the thought had a low growl escaping his throat.

The situation with Rose surprised him. Not that Delilah had taken a swipe at one of his deputies, but the timing. Maybe Rose had just been in the wrong place at the wrong time.

Or had Delilah planned this around his run for re-election? He wouldn't be surprised. What did surprise him was the fact that she'd managed to control a half-change. And that had to be what she was doing. It was rare and it was powerful. He'd only heard of a handful of shifters that could do it. Part wolf. Part human. Even the wolf in him chilled.

The slamming of the front door and the stomping of boots brought him out of his preoccupation. Delaney. He'd know that step anywhere. She'd be in the office in four, three, two...

The door flew open. She came in wearing a scowl. "I thought I'd go out and check on old man Stone's wolfdogs."

He gave her a quizzical look. "Well hello to you too. I expected you to come in wearing the expression of a kitty cat that just got fed cream."

Her scowl deepened. She took a belligerent stance, her thumbs stuck in the front of her pants. "Oh yeah, and why would that be?"

"I thought the real deal would be a big improvement over phone sex."

She flopped into the chair in front of the desk and stared at the picture of a misty mountain scene behind his head. A Christmas gift from Rose.

"There's some nasty strings attached," she muttered, kicking the heels of her boots against the chair.

"Like what?"

"He wants to get married."

For a moment everything inside of him stilled, including his heartbeat. He forced himself to say lightly, "The bastard."

"I like my life."

"You're an odd one, Delaney. Most women would be turning cartwheels at a marriage offer."

"Would you be?" she shot back.

"If Hanigan offered for me I'd deck him."

"Exactly." She nodded vigorously then shot him a scathing look as she got his joke. "Very funny."

"Do you love him?" His breath stuck in his lungs as he waited her response.

"I like him. He's good in bed." She jumped up like a jack in the box and began to pace.

"I'm not sure that's enough to base a marriage on," he replied in a dry voice once he had some air. "Even car rods stop working when they get enough age on them."

"Har de har."

"How long is he here for?"

Her head shot up and her eyes widened. "I have no idea. I forgot to ask."

Mateo snorted. "He does have you rattled."

She made a chopping motion in the air. "Enough about my sex life. You got any problems with me paying Stone a visit?"

"Nope."

Her gaze drilled him and she said shrewdly, "But you think it's a waste of time. Why?"

"Just my gut. But if nothing else it will eliminate his wolfdogs."

She started pacing again. As she passed his desk, her gaze fell on the drawing and she stopped. "You know her, don't you?"

He started to deny it then heaved a sigh. What was the point? "For my sins. What name is she going by?"

"Layla Sosa."

"She was Delilah Devon when I knew her."

"She does look like a Delilah." She fingered a loose strand of hair. "You think she's behind the attacks?"

"I wouldn't rule it out." He had to tread carefully. He could hardly tell his pragmatic deputy that Delilah was a shifter. He rubbed his chin. Though, not as pragmatic as she liked to believe. Pragmatists didn't have spidey senses.

"Well, we know Jesse wouldn't listen to you, if he'd even talk to you. Want me to give it a go?"

He flashed her a quick grin. "I appreciate that, Delaney." Then he sobered. "But at this point, he wouldn't listen to you either. He's enthralled."

"How do you know?"

"I'm not dissing your powers of persuasion, but I've been there. I know her appeal." He made a dismissive motion with his hand.

"Well, she does have that in spades," Blair admitted and dropped back in the chair. "Why, do you think she's behind the attacks? And how?"

"I said I wouldn't rule her out. And how is the question, isn't it?" Even though he had a damn good idea.

"Did you part on bad terms?"

"You could say that. Why?"

"To be so smart, there are times you can be really obtuse. But then you're a guy."

"Okay, we've established that I'm smart, obtuse and a guy. What's your point?"

"It's election year." She leaned back in her chair and waited for it to sink in.

"You think these attacks are to get at me?" Hadn't he been thinking along the same lines? It all coalesced and made a chilling kind of sense.

"If you can't stop the attacks your re-election is hardly a shoe-in. How about if after I talk to Stone I head over to the rez, see what I can dig up?"

"Delaney, I don't want you anywhere near her and that's an order." He drilled her with a hard gaze.

Her fists clenched. "You think she attacked Rose, don't you?"

"Just stay away from her. I'll take care of this."

"You know there are places that make high-end cosmetic dental prosthetics. I'm sure she could have some made to slide in and out. Same for the nails. Is she that crazy?"

"Cunning. She's that cunning."

"You must have really pissed her off."

"You could say that."

"You want to tell me about it?"

He stood up. "You go check on Stone. I think I'll swing by and check on Rose."

"That would be a no then." She gave him a quirky smile. "No need to check on Rose. Quinn walked in when I did. He threw his crooner charm around and got her released this morning. Says she's doing fine. He plans on taking her dinner after work. I believe I smell a romance."

"Rose and Quinn? Now that's a scary thought." Mateo blinked.

"How could you have missed it. He's had a crush on her for ages."

"Quinn?"

"And here I thought you were so observant." She shook her head and sauntered out.

"Apparently, I'm not," he muttered to the room at large.

CHAPTER 13

Blair sat at her silver-finished vanity—a gift from her momma—and slicked scarlet lipstick on her generous mouth, as Luke lazed in bed, his blonde hair rumpled, his chest bare and his expression satisfied. She flashed him a wicked grin and picked up a red dangling earring.

"Looking good, babe. Hope I'm not going to have to fight off a bunch of horny males. Where are we going by the way?"

"The local watering hole on the rez." She fastened the earrings then wiggled into black skinny jeans.

He watched with an appreciative gleam in his eyes. "Any particular reason?"

"Just wanted to give you some local color. You're the one thinking about moving to Billings." She pulled on a low-cut red blouse.

"You never mentioned what your thoughts were on that."

She reached for black boots that worked for dress up or down. "You need to make up your mind on that and leave me out of the equation."

"You're half of the equation and the reason I'm considering the move."

She shoved her feet into the boots and stood up. "I don't want to talk about this now. Let's just go and have a good time, okay?"

He didn't agree or disagree just changed the subject. "Does going to the rez have anything to do with your war paint?"

"I beg your pardon?"

"Other than painting your toenails with the wildest colors you can find, you are usually more subdued in your makeup and clothes. If I wasn't going with you, I'd think you were on the make."

Her back went up and her eyebrows lowered.

He ignored the look and went on. "Which leaves me to wonder if we are going undercover."

She sashayed over to him and placed her crimson lips on his then wiped off the lipstick with her thumb. "Aren't you the astute one. You know Rose was attacked?"

"You mentioned that. Too bad. I like Rose. She's a nice woman." He threw back the sheets and reached for his pants.

"Yes, she is." Her skin tightened. She clenched and unclenched her fists. Then realizing what she was doing, forced herself to relax.

"And you think it's someone on the rez?" He stood up, zipped his pants and reached for a white button up shirt.

"I think it's a definite possibility."

"Is the sheriff going to be there?" he asked with a definite lack of enthusiasm.

She laughed. "Mateo is persona non grata on the

rez."

"Why is that?"

"He and the police chief, don't get along." Before he could ask, she continued, "I have no idea why. I don't think anyone does. Apparently, they were pretty close growing up."

"Too bad. I was looking forward to spending more time with him."

"You are such a liar." She chuckled.

"So, who are we looking for?"

Blair turned serious. "I'd like to get your opinion without me biasing it. And sh—, the person of interest may not even be there."

"You think it's a woman. Hence the war paint." He nodded and gave her a knowing smile.

"I didn't say that."

"You don't have to. I know you better than you think."

"Maybe not as well as you think you do."

He strolled over, nuzzled her neck and ran a finger lightly along the inside of her thigh. "I know you."

Her breath caught and her heart jumped. "You got me there." She gave him a light shove and glanced at the clock. "Eight o'clock on a week night. It's going to be early action instead of late. We better boogie."

He tucked his shirt into his pants. "Let's do it."

~*~

Drums and an electric guitar reverberated as Luke and Blair wove their way through the crowd on the dance floor and headed to the bar. Tribal memorabilia fought for space with local beer signs and a large mirror on the pine wall behind a gleaming wood counter.

Jerry, a young Blackfoot, rode the stick. Blair held up two fingers. He smiled, nodded and filled two mugs. She lifted up on her toes, trying to see if Jesse and Delilah were here. It was Wednesday. The night the local band Full Moon played. Like herself, Jesse was a fan. They both showed up for a few hours whenever they could get away. They'd missed each other for a full month now.

Jerry shot two beers down the gleaming counter. One stopped in front of her. The other within inches of it. She took a sip of her beer. Looked like tonight was going to be another miss.

She handed Luke his brew and shouted above the crowd. "There's one booth left. Let's snag it before someone else does." They snaked through the crowd and had nearly reached the table when Luke stopped short. She trod on his heels and had to grab the beer with both hands to keep it from spilling. "What?"

"Who the hell is that?"

She followed his gaze and saw Delilah and Jesse. Satisfaction zinged through her. She gave him a light shove. "Keep moving. They're after our table."

When he still didn't move, she gave his rear a pinch. "Move it, Detective."

He jumped and his beer spilled on his hand and splashed on a nearby male who cursed him.

"Sorry." He shoved his way through and they arrived at the table at the same time as Jesse and

Delilah.

Blair thumped her beer down on the table in a show of ownership.

"Hey, Blair." Jesse shot Luke a curious glance. "I don't believe we've met."

Blair gave Luke a sharp jab to the ribs with her elbow.

Luke tore his gaze away from Delilah who he'd been staring at, with a glazed expression on his face, put down his beer and stuck out his hand. "Luke Hanigan."

Jesse shook it. "I haven't seen you around here before."

"I'm from Atlanta. I'm with the Atlanta PD."

"Ah, the boyfriend." He put his arm around Delilah.

"This is Layla Sosa."

"Detective." Layla/Delilah held out her hand.

Luke took it. His eyes widened and his jaw dropped.

He looked positively moronic. If he didn't get his act together, Blair was going to drop kick him across the dance floor.

"She has that effect." Jesse gave Blair an apologetic shrug, though pride shone in his eyes and on the small smile that played on his face. "Mind if we share the booth?"

"Not at all." Perfect. She slid in followed by Luke.

"So, Lana, getting settled in?" She took a sip of her beer.

"That's Layla, Officer." The black-haired beauty

SANDRA COX

gave her a fake smile.

"My mistake. And it's Chief Deputy."

Jesse glanced from one to the other then shifted as if in discomfort on the hard bench.

Layla snapped her fingers. "Oh, that's right. You work for...."

"Mateo Grey."

"Oh yes, I've heard of him."

"I'm sure. He's laid nearly everyone in the county."

"Does that include you, Chief Deputy?" Layla all but purred.

Luke stiffened, apparently coming out of the sexual haze Layla so easily wove.

"Let's just say we're close enough I know about his past indiscretions." She gave a knowing smile. If Luke had stiffened before, he'd turned into wood now. She elbowed him to remind him they were undercover, but it didn't seem to help. At least it might have dropped the scales from Jesse's eyes, the way his gaze had narrowed momentarily on Layla/Delilah before he got his game face on.

"Let's dance." Luke scooted out of the booth. Before she could say yea or nay, he pulled her onto the dance floor, causing her to slosh her beer as she thumped it on the table.

"What was that about?" he shouted over the buzz of voices from the dance floor.

"What the hell are you talking about, Hanigan?" She tried to pull back but his grip held. She gave some thought to decking him, but there wasn't enough room to draw her arm back.

134

"You and Mateo? I knew it."

"I beg your pardon?" Her voice iced as did her heart before anger exploded in heated furious waves. She tried again to push away. When he just held on tighter, she put her forearm between them and pried him away.

"You and Mateo. You basically told her you had or were," he emphasized the were, "sleeping with that macho bastard."

"And I told you I was working undercover, trying to get under her skin, which it appears I did." She bit the words out.

They stood in the middle of the dance floor glaring at each other as couples danced around them, occasionally bumping into them.

"That's your idea of going undercover? Baiting that woman? And what makes you think it's her? Because she oozes sexuality like a bitch in heat?" Unfortunately, the band chose that moment to take a break. People around them tittered.

Blair turned on her heel and headed toward the booth. Seeing it was empty, she switched direction and headed outside. She'd done what she came to do. Even if it had made her boyfriend look like a flaming jackass.

"Wait."

She kept up her long-legged pace, heading for the SUV.

"Blair, wait."

She jumped in the driver's seat and gunned the engine. Before she could throw it in gear, Luke hopped in. She tore out. When a young woman leaped out of her way, she slowed and rolled down the window trying to cool the red-hot poker pushing at her brain.

Luke rolled down his window too. Neither spoke for five miles. Finally, he said, "I'm sorry, Delaney."

She didn't respond.

"That woman packs a powerful dose of something." He rubbed his chin.

"Sex appeal?" A corner of her lip went up in a sneer.

"No more than you, babe."

She snorted.

"No, it's more than that. It's almost evil. She had me ready to tear out Grey's throat and while I'm not a fan, I'm also not a rampaging, rutting bull moose."

Somewhat appeased she gave him an almost smile. "Could have fooled me. And I mean that in the best possible way."

He leaned over and gave her knee a light rub. "I know there's nothing between you and Grey. If for no other reason than you'd never be a notch on anyone's belt."

"You got that right." She glanced over and flashed a grin.

"Watch out." The fingers on her knee bit in painfully.

Her eyes back on the road, she stomped on the brakes. The tires locked as the big car skidded, stopping inches from the black wolf that stood in the middle of the road.

The hair on the back of her neck rose as glowing

green eyes stared into hers. The contact seemed to last forever till the wolf with an arrogant toss of its head disappeared into the inky-black trees that lined the road.

"Jesus, Mary and Joseph, what was that?"

It took several attempts to swallow past her dry throat. "Appears to have been a wolf." She tapped the pedal and the vehicle rolled forward at a sedate pace. Her gaze constantly checking the road and the sides of the road.

"This is one crazy place. Come back to Atlanta with me, Blair. It's not safe for you here."

"We're police officers, Luke. It's not safe for us anywhere." She gave a humorless laugh.

Before he could respond, his phone rang. "Hanigan." He listened for a moment. "Really? Okay. Yeah. Tomorrow." He shoved the phone back in his pocket.

"There's been a break in a case I'm working on. I've got to fly back. How about you come back with me? You know Atlanta PD would snap you back up in a heartbeat."

"I can't do that."

"Can't or won't?"

"Doesn't matter."

"How can you stand the cold?"

She laughed. "That I'm still getting used to."

"At least think about it, okay?"

"Sure."

They both knew she'd already made up her mind.

Later that night, after they'd exhausted

themselves in each other, she lay awake unable to sleep, watching the moon travel across the sky. A brisk breeze, from the window cracked an inch, raised goosebumps on bare skin.

A wolf howled. Close. Menacing.

She jumped out of bed and raced to the window. It stood several yards away. Watching. Waiting. She grabbed her rifle and headed for the door. When she got there, it melted into the darkness. She backed into the house, unwilling to show fear, as her heart beat hard and fast. She shut and locked the door, leaned against it and closed her eyes. What in sweet hell was going on?

CHAPTER 14

6:45 AM.

Mateo stared at the white-faced, black-numbered clock on the wall. With the exception of LeRoy, the night dispatcher, who sat at his desk waiting for Quinn to relieve him, the station stood empty, his crew not due in till eight.

The door to the outer office opened and closed.

Footsteps. Then a knock.

"Come in."

Surprise darted through his system when he looked up. "Hanigan."

"Grey." Luke nodded.

"What can I do for you?" Mateo motioned toward the chair in front of his desk.

Luke shook his head. "I can't stay. I'm on my way to the airport."

"Leaving already?"

"I had a case that took a twist. I need to get back."

"I get it." He nodded. "What can I do for you?"

Luke looked uncomfortable and shifted on his feet. "I know it goes with the job, but I'm a little concerned about Blair."

"You're going to have to be more specific."

"There's something weird going on around here."

Mateo stiffened. "Again. You're going to have to be more specific."

"We went to the Blue Coyote last night."

"Full Moon playing?"

"Yeah, they're pretty good."

"Yes, they are. But what does Full Moon playing at the Blue Coyote have to do with your concern for Blair?"

"We went specifically because Blair wanted to check on Layla Sosa."

Blood roared in Mateo's ears. He managed not to grind his teeth. "I told Delaney to stay away from her."

"That definitely wasn't the impression I got. What's with that chick anyway?"

Mateo rose to his feet trying to beat back his horror. Delaney had no idea who she was messing with. "Which chick?"

"The hot one."

Mateo cocked an eyebrow.

Luke made a dismissing motion. "Delaney's plenty hot but it doesn't ooze out of her pores. She did everything she could to get Layla's back up. And she used you to do it."

This time he did grind his teeth. "I'll definitely have a little chat with her."

"That woman's dangerous. Ever smelled evil?"

He had but was surprised that Luke was capable of it, which just went to show how dangerous Delilah truly was.

"Yes."

"She reeks of it. And another odd thing. A black wolf stepped out in the middle of the road on our way home. I swear it stared straight at Blair. I don't spook easily but it spooked me." He glanced at his watch. "I gotta go. You'll keep an eye on her? Rein her in?"

"Count on it."

"I'll probably pay for sticking my nose in." Luke's expression grew rueful.

"I'll keep you out of it, if I can."

"Appreciate it." He gave a mini salute and was gone.

Mateo sunk down in his chair. He was going to wring Delaney's lovely neck. What had she been thinking having a pissing contest with Delilah? Delaney was as stubborn as a mule when she got an idea in her head and she wanted justice for Rose. Hell, he did too. But he was the one that was going to mete it out. He had no desire to be visiting Delaney in the hospital or the morgue. Cold beads of sweat slicked his skin. Not on his watch. He had to get Delilah off the reservation and deal with her before the attacks escalated and someone died.

He picked up the top piece of paper in the pile on the center of his desk. It was why he came in early, to get the damn paperwork done. When he'd stared at it for several minutes without anything registering, he threw it down in disgust and began to pace.

Once again, the outer door slammed. He recognized the clop of Delaney's boots. Looked like she was in early too. He'd barely settled behind the desk when she managed to elbow open the door while holding two cups with Belle's Beans printed on their sides. The aromatic scent notched down the cold anger knotting his gut. But not enough.

She placed one on his desk. "Figured you'd rather have this than Quinn's."

"Quinn here?"

"Yeah. Beat me by five minutes."

"LeRoy's already gone?"

"Yeah, he doesn't waste any time once Quinn hits the door."

"Umm." He took a sip of his coffee and his fury notched back to manageable proportions. He no longer had the urge to jump across the desk and shake his chief deputy till her teeth rattled.

She slumped in the chair and yawned widely. Dark craters circled her eyes. The skin on her cheeks stretched tight across the bones and she rubbed between her eyes with her index finger the way she did when she had a headache.

"What's up?"

"What makes you think anything's up?" She straightened.

"Cut the crap. You look like hell."

"Thanks for that."

He waited.

She took another sip of coffee, set it back down and cleared her throat. "You know a lot about wolves."

The hair on the back of his neck rose. He waited.

Finally, she spit it out. "Do they track people?" She cringed after she said it as if she expected him to laugh at her.

"Why are you asking?"

"One jumped in front of my car last night and seemed to be staring straight at me. Then early this morning, one howled outside the cabin." She rubbed her arms then jumped up and paced, just as he had not so long ago. "Coincidence, right?"

"What road were you on when the wolf jumped in front of your car?"

"We were coming back from the Blue Coyote," she said without thinking then cleared her throat as she realized she might have said more than she should.

"Full Moon playing?" He asked it casually as if he were just making conversation.

"Yeah."

"If I remember that's Kipp's favorite band. Was he there?"

"Yeah." She drummed her fingers against her thighs.

"Anyone with him?"

She didn't answer.

He waited.

The silence stretched. Tension built.

Finally, she threw herself back into the chair. "Fine. Yes, Layla was there. We think she hurt Rose remember?"

He leaped to his feet and shot around the desk. Swinging her chair around, he leaned down in her face, close enough to smell the coffee on her breath and the citrus scent that permeated her skin as sharp and tangy as her personality. "I remember all right. Do you remember what I told you about staying away from Delilah Devon?"

"She hurt Rose. I'm sure of it." She gave him stare for stare.

"And how do you plan to prove it?"

She stuck her chin in the air, her expression pugnacious.

His wolf stirred restlessly. Anger rose. "You plan on using yourself for bait don't you? Rile her till she comes after you?"

She stared back, mutinous.

Something snapped. He grabbed her collar and hauled her to her feet till there was no distance between them.

Her eyes widened.

His wolf pushed. Desire stirred.

They stared at each other. His head dropped, ready to kiss her into compliance when a knock sounded at the door. He dropped his hands, took an unhurried step back when Quinn stuck his head in. He looked back and forth between them curiously. Tension and desire lingered in the air.

"I can come back if I'm interrupting anything."

"You're not. What's up?"

"I just wanted to give you an update on Rose. She's doing fine and plans to come back tomorrow. She would have been here today if I hadn't insisted she take another day."

It appeared Delaney had been right on her assessment of Quinn's feelings for Rose. He couldn't imagine two more different people, but when it came to love and longing, compatibility didn't always factor in.

Delaney took advantage of the conversation to slip out the door.

"Delaney," he bellowed.

She stuck her head back in, her expression wary.

"We aren't done. Please sit down."

He could tell, she longed to tell him where to go. Only the fact that he was her boss prevented it. His lips twitched.

"Thanks, Quinn." His eyes stayed on Delaney.

Quinn mumbled something and let himself out.

"You go against a direct order again and I'll bench you."

"You are shorthanded as it is."

"Without pay."

"Then I'll just do it on my own."

He heaved a sigh and ran restless fingers through his hair. "What am I supposed to do with you? I'm telling you that woman is dangerous."

"It's part of the job."

"I am equipped to deal with her better than you are."

She lifted her lips in an elegant sneer. "Why? Because you have a penis? That is so sexist."

He grinned and began to relax. "It sounds that way doesn't it? Let's just say I know more about her than you do, including her weaknesses. Leave it with me."

She didn't respond. He fought the urge to shake her. The alpha in him had a strong desire to show his dominance. The man knew she would do what she thought right, come hell or high water.

"You're over your head Delaney. You can't begin to conceive Delilah's abilities. You are dealing with forces beyond your comprehension."

"Abilities? Forces?"

He'd said too much. His gaze drilled into her as if he could make her listen by sheer force of will.

She gave a clipped nod. "Is that all?"

"Yes." This time he didn't stop her when she bolted out the door, leaving the scent of fear and fury behind.

~*~

Ten o'clock.

Blair mindlessly flipped channels on her small flat screen TV. Finding nothing of interest, she tossed down the control and began to pace. She stopped in front of the rickety bookcase she'd found at a secondhand store and picked up a silver-framed photo. The full moon shone through the window and haloed the frame. She and her mother smiled into the camera. It had been taken at one of the endless charity events her mother organized. They were both dressed to the nines, wearing stilettoes and carrying glittering evening bags.

Her mother and she had nothing in common and didn't understand each other. But they loved one another dearly and that came through in the photograph. She put it down and strode to the window.

She'd been edgy all evening. Between Luke's unexpected suggestion of marriage—you couldn't call it a proposal—the run in with that bitch Layla-Delilah, the black wolf in the road and last but not least that moment when Mateo hauled her up against him with that gleam in his eye that said as clearly as words, he planned to kiss her senseless, she had a right to be.

She'd always known he packed a potent amount of sex appeal, but she'd never gotten it turned on her up close and personal. Just thinking about it had her knees wobbling. She reached for the windowsill to steady herself, looked smack into glowing green eyes and screamed like a girl.

The wolf stood on her porch, its black fur gleaming in the moonlight. At her reaction, it drew back its lips in a wolfish smile. It was smaller than the wolf that hung around Mateo's place. The frame more slender.

She slammed back against the wall, her heart hammering, her breathing uneven. Then bulleted to the catchall table beside the door, jerked open the drawer and yanked out her Glock. Gun raised, pulse racing she threw open the door and stepped onto the porch.

Where was the wolf?

She did a slow 180 from left to right. "Where are you, you bastard?"

A low growl sounded in the dark. The hair on the back of her neck lifted and she whirled toward the sound. Nothing, past the porch light's muted yellow glow, but darkness. "Come on out, you four-legged horror."

The growl came again, deep in the grove of oak at the edge of the property. Why the hell hadn't she grabbed her flashlight? She took one step off the porch and stopped. She wasn't getting in a pissing match with a wolf in the dark. The wind picked up and a screech owl screamed to her left causing her to jump and swivel in that direction.

A hot furry body hit her from behind and knocked her down. The gun went off as it fell from her fingers. Hot breath fanned the side of her face. A long tongue licked along the side of her neck. Claws dug into her shoulders.

Just like Opel and Rose, except Opel thought a human had attacked her. She must have been mistaken.

The fangs dug in delicately splitting the skin. Desperately, she reached for the gun. The wolf growled and bit into her upper arm.

"Son of a bitch." She shrieked in pain.

The wolf transferred its fangs back to her neck and bit down. Hot blood spurted. This was it. She was going to die an ignominious death at the hands of a maddened wolf. Rabies. Maybe it had rabies. Animals didn't carry out vendettas. Or maybe it had developed a taste for human blood.

No by God, she wasn't going to die like this. She began to flail, trying to shake it off. She hit out with her good arm. The wolf growled and bit deeper. Blood spurted. She hit out again and the wolf went flying.

Her vision blurred. One wolf had become two. Loss of blood? Concussion? She blinked. For a moment the images snapped into place. The black wolf fought a large gray and black wolf that seemed hell bent on tearing it to pieces. Wobbly, she reached for her gun. Her arm trembled as she aimed at the moving, snarling targets then pulled the trigger.

The black wolf yipped and raced off limping. The gray wolf looked from her to the black wolf then trotted toward her. She raised the gun but her strength was gone. It dropped from her nerveless fingers.

"Go ahead and rip my throat out you hairy bastard. I'm too damn tired to care." The wolf whimpered and licked her cheek.

The next moment Mateo was leaning over her. "Come on, Delaney, stay with me." His voice brisk, his hands all over her.

"How did you get here?" She managed to pry open matted eyes. "Where's your clothes?"

"You're hallucinating, Delaney."

He carefully pulled off her shirt.

"Not tonight, honey. I've got a headache." She laughed then began to cough then choke. Blood spurted from her neck.

"Don't talk." He laid her shirt against her throat then put her hand on it. "Hold this on. I'll be right back."

Weirder and weirder, she'd somehow managed to fall down Alice's rabbit hole.

The cloth under her hand grew damp. She needed to focus, apply pressure, but she was so very tired. Her head lolled to the side, her cheek resting against cold loamy earth.

Arms circled her and she floated upward, pressed

against a hot chest and a fast-beating heart. A new cloth pressed against her neck.

"You still don't have your clothes on." Her arms dangled at her sides.

"Don't worry, Delaney, I've got my jeans on. That's as decent as it gets." He packed her into her SUV. She floated in and out as he turned on the siren.

~*~

Mateo stomped the pedal to the floor. Thank goodness he'd had the presence of mind to leave a change of clothes on the outskirts of her tiny property when he heard about her being stalked by a black wolf. Delilah, of course.

"Hang on, Delaney." He picked up the handheld on the radio. "This is Grey, I'm taking Delaney straight to the clinic. Have someone standing by and have a transfusion ready. O negative. I'll be there soon."

"Ten-four."

One hand on the steering wheel, he drew on his shirt with the other.

It should have taken twenty minutes but he made it in eleven. Thank the powers that be, no one else was on the road except a pickup that had the good sense to pull to the side when the driver saw the flashers. Nor some hapless four-legged critter.

He pulled under the clinic's awning, raced to the passenger side and pulled her into his arms. He'd barely taken two steps forward when Nurse Evangeline Szoke, Jerome's mom, came bulleting at him, pushing a gurney.

He laid Delaney on it.

"What happened?"

"Wolf attack. She needs blood and stitches." He arranged Delaney in the center of the already moving gurney.

"A wolf attack? Do you think it was rabid?" She arrowed the gurney through the double glass doors. A clear plastic bag of blood attached.

"Don't think so. Just a rogue black wolf." He strode beside the gurney holding the blood-soaked shirt in place at her neck.

"We don't have black wolves around here."

"It was black."

She wheeled the gurney into one of the three rooms used for overnights. He glanced at the yellow walls and the painting of a mountain scene. Same room Rose had been in.

"What can I do?" His chest rose and fell with each breath. His heart continued to beat which surprised him since his innards had turned to ice.

"Just what you're doing." She swabbed one of Delaney's flaccid arms then inserted a needle, taped it down and started the transfusion.

Even with the blood flowing into her system, color continued to leach from Delaney's skin. "Where's the damn doctor?" His voice sounded as dry and gritty as his throat.

"On his way. Should be here in—" She glanced at her plain, large-lettered watch. "Five minutes."

"She may not have five minutes." His hand wet and red from the blood seeping through the cloth.

She glanced at his face then at the blood dripping through his fingers and with her no-nonsense stride came around the side of the bed, gently nudged him away, removed the bloody cloth and applied a wide gauze pad from the bedside tray to the wound. "Don't you worry, Sheriff. We aren't losing her on my watch."

The door swung open and Dr. Greene bulleted through. He strode to the sink and scrubbed his hands. A white jacket covered worn jeans and a faded brown Grizzlies jersey. If the doc had reached thirty—Mateo's age—Mateo would be surprised. Still in all, Greene was competent and caring. A good combination in his book.

He slipped on a pair of gloves. "Evangeline. Sheriff." He nodded, his gaze locked on the patient. "What've we got?"

"It's Blair Delaney, Doc. She needs stitches stat. She's pumping like a geyser." Evangeline pushed a tray toward the bed with suture clamps and a round threaded needle.

Greene gave a nod of approval. "Let's do this." He glanced at Mateo. "Maybe you better leave, Sheriff."

"I'm not going anywhere."

"Just don't faint. We don't have an extra pair of hands to take care of you too."

"I've seen blood before."

"You're as white as the patient."

"She's my chief deputy." Nothing more needed to be said. She was one of his.

"Alright then. Continue pressing. Evangeline, get more gauze pads."

"Right away, Doctor." She bustled out.

The doc stepped up beside Mateo. "I need to get a look at that wound."

He cautiously pulled back the bloody pad. "What the hell did this?"

"A wolf."

Evangeline came bustling in and ripped open a new pad for the doc. He tossed the old one into the trash and placed the new one over the wound.

"It looks like he tried to rip her throat out."

"It does."

The doc cast a quick look at Mateo's set face then turned his attention back to his patient. "Evangeline, keep pressure on one end of the wound while I work on the other."

Once again, Mateo found himself bumped out of the way. With quick sure movements, the doc began to sew. Mateo lost track of the times the needle flashed in and out.

"Another pad, Sheriff," Evangeline directed.

With clumsy fingers, he ripped open another gauze pad.

Finally, the doc put away the needle and sterilized the area. Once, twice and yet again. "That should do it."

"She's going to be alright?" Anxiety, from the wolf, coursed through his system. He kept it at bay by sheer force of will. It moved restlessly inside him, eager to be set free, to throw back its head and howl. And then hunt. Hunt down the black wolf and destroy it. Blood lust still up, barely contained below the surface.

"No reason why she shouldn't. She lost a lot of blood. I'd give her a couple of weeks to re-cooperate. Maybe have her ride the desk. She can be released tomorrow morning, if she's feeling alright."

Evangeline snorted. Her eyes met Mateo's and he shook his head.

"What?" The doc's eyes, a soft blue behind wide frames, narrowed.

"Perhaps, you could keep her at the clinic for a couple of days," Mateo suggested.

Evangeline nodded vigorously. "It's a good idea. Doc?"

"Are you trying to tell me keeping her down would be difficult?" Doc snapped off his gloves and threw them in the trash.

"Might as well try to stop the wind from blowing. That child only knows one speed and it's fast." Evangeline picked up the tray with the medical utensils on it.

"Then we'll keep her a couple of nights."

"Thanks, Doc." Mateo reached out his big callused paw and shook Doc's smaller one, cracked from constant scrubbing.

"Not a problem. I'll be by tomorrow morning." He looked out the window at the pinkening sky. "Later this morning," he corrected himself.

Mateo dropped into the nearby chair and yawned.

"Short night?" Evangeline asked.

"They don't get much shorter." He studied the plastic bag, with the clear liquid drip, hanging near the blood bag. "Something to knock her out?"

"She needs her sleep. As do you. Why don't you go home?"

"I don't want her to wake up by herself."

"Our Blair is tough. She's got Jerome walking the straight and narrow. For which I'm eternally grateful."

Mateo chuckled. "She is that. Still I don't want her to wake up alone."

"You're a good man, Sheriff. You've got my vote in the upcoming election. And everyone else's that I know of as well."

"Thanks, Evangeline. I appreciate that."

She dropped a hand briefly on his shoulder then hustled out, starched uniform rustling.

He settled in an ancient tan recliner whose handle stuck, shifting away from a loose coil biting him in the butt. He gently touched Delaney's hand. She murmured and wrapped her fingers around his but didn't wake. He looked at their entwined hands. Something in him softened and the tension riding him fell away. He told himself he was just comfort in the dark, she didn't know whose hand she held. Still he didn't let go.

His one attempt at a relationship with one of his kind had been a disaster. Beauty and sensuality had hidden cruelty and horror. At that point, he knew his life would be as a loner. He didn't dare share his secret with a human and if Delilah was any example of his kind, he was better off alone.

Still holding her hand, he leaned back and closed his eyes.

Someone shook his shoulders. "Boss."

SANDRA COX

He blinked, staring into Rose's warm brown eyes.

"I'll take over. Go home and get some sleep."

"What time is it?"

"Seven."

His hand was numb and his arm tingled were it had fallen asleep. He looked at Delaney's hand wrapped around his. Even with discomfort shooting up his arm, he was loath to let go.

"I'll look after her, Boss."

Rose's tan shirt and brown pants fit her a little looser than they normally did and a long scratch that ran down the side of her face hadn't quite healed. "I appreciate you checking on me while I was in the hospital and when I was home."

"Sorry it wasn't more often. Sorry it happened at all. I plan to get to the bottom of this."

"I don't doubt it for a minute."

He worked his hand free from Delaney's with care. Then pushed out of the chair and stretched.

"What happened?"

"She was attacked by a black wolf. Do you still think a person attacked you?"

She shook her head causing graying, blonde curls to dance. "I just don't know. It's so surreal. Makes me think I'm crazy. I saw a human in the distance, but it was definitely a slobbering mad dog or wolf that had at me. I could feel its hot breath on my neck." Her eyes glazed over. Fear filled them. A shudder shook her.

"Don't worry. We'll get to the bottom of it." He put a reassuring hand on her shoulder.

She nodded and pointed at the tray. "I brought you

a cup of coffee from The Bean. I had them make it decaf so you'd be able to catch a few hours before you go in. I told Quinn you'd be in around noon. Don't make a liar of me by going straight to the station."

He threw up his hands in surrender. "I know when I've been bested. So, when did you speak to Quinn?"

A blush settled over her round face. "He's insisted on staying at my place to make sure I'm alright. Completely unnecessary, of course." She watched his twitching lips and hurried to add. "He sleeps on the couch."

"I'm glad you've got someone to take care of you." He grabbed his decaf with a definite lack of enthusiasm. Saluted her with it and left.

CHAPTER 15

Her eyes heavy, she floated toward consciousness. Instead of soft worn sheets, cool crisp ones touched her body. Instead of the scents of coffee and stale pizza, the acrid smell of cleaners and alcohol burned her nostrils. Her neck hurt like a mother and when she moved her hand her skin pinched and pulled.

What the hell?

Memory raised an insidious head before flattening her. That damn scary black wolf. It had lured her out of the house and tried to kill her. Probably would have succeeded if the silver and black wolf hadn't attacked it. A wolf with Mateo's unusual amber eyes. And then Mateo himself. A naked Mateo. Surely, that memory wasn't right. Though it was seared on her brain. Everything else ran together. Fuzzy. Unreal. The wolf ripping at her throat.

She lay flat on her back gasping for air.

"Blair. Blair honey, are you alright?"

Rose's concerned voice reached her and brought her back from the precipice of run-for-your-life fear that threatened to engulf her. Rose. If anyone would understand, Rose would. Blindly, she held out a hand.

Rose grasped it, hers warm against the ice of her

own.

She forced her eyes open and promptly closed them.

"Blair. It's okay, honey."

She blew out the trapped air in her lungs and blinked. "I was hoping it was a nightmare. You know what it felt like right?"

"Yes, honey. I do." Rose squeezed her hand.

"How did I get here?"

"Do you remember anything?"

"Fuzzy flashes."

"Mateo brought you in."

Mateo naked, with blood under his fingernails and a trickle on his mouth. No. That made no more sense than him being naked. She moved her head restlessly. "Where is he?"

"I sent him home." Rose's eyes filled. For one panicked moment Blair feared her friend would start crying. "What's wrong?"

"When I came in, he was asleep, holding your hand."

"Excuse me?" If she hadn't been wired up to tubes, she would have put her finger in her ear and shook it. Surely, she'd heard wrong.

"Mateo. When I got here, he was sleeping in the chair holding your hand."

Warmth flooded her system and she bit back a silly smile. "So, the tough guy has a soft side."

"Haven't I always told you?"

"Yes, and I'll be the first to admit, neither I nor anyone else believed you."

"Well, he has."

Before Rose could say more the door swished open and Pearl—the nurse on duty—sailed in, clipboard in hand. She carried a few extra pounds, smelled of roses and sanitizer and barely topped five two.

"I see we're awake." The eternal we that nurses used. "How do we feel?"

"Like we," she emphasized sarcastically, "had a tire iron taken to us."

"A little grumpy, huh? Would you like some pain meds?" Pearl peeled back the bandage at her throat, looked at it, then put a clean one on.

Rose slipped through the door, mouthing, "I'll be back."

Blair nodded then turned her attention to Pearl. "How bad is it?"

"It's going to heal and you are going to be fine. If the sheriff hadn't got you in when he did—" She shook her head.

Once again, a glimpse of a silver and black magnificent-looking wolf flashed in her mind, followed by a picture of a just-as-magnificent naked Mateo. She rubbed her forehead and really wished she could lose that image.

Pearl took her temperature, blood pressure and checked the bag of nutrients attached to her arm.

"Any chance, I can lose that thing?" She hated needles, especially ones stuck in her. They made her twitch.

"The doc will be in later this morning. I'll ask him."

"Thanks, Pearl."

Pearl patted her shoulder and left.

Ten minutes later, the door swished opened and Rose came back in carrying a Bean's cup and a Bean's sack.

Blair's stomach growled in response. She pushed up in bed and reached out with her unhampered hand. "You're the best, Rose."

"I'm sure they'll be by with your breakfast but this will tide you over till they do." Rose winked.

"How come you never married, Rose? You are such a nurturer. You should have a dozen children to cosset."

"I've got the whole county to take care of. Who'd have the time?" She made a dismissive gesture with her hand.

Blair awkwardly opened the bag.

"Here let me do that for you." She unwrapped a bacon, egg and cheese bagel and handed it to Blair.

Blair took a bite large enough to make her mother wince if she'd been there to see it.

"What happened, hon?" Rose sat down in the ancient recliner and picked at a small hole in the worn fabric on the arm.

"Wolf attacked me," she mumbled around a bite-full then swallowed. "You too, right?"

"I'm still wrestling with that one," Rose admitted, rubbing her arm. "The breath on my cheek, the fangs, the claws, all wolf. But I saw a shadowy figure that I'd swear was a man or a woman."

"You never mentioned a woman before." Blair

straightened in bed and set down her bagel.

Before Rose could say more, the door swung open.

"Well crap," Blair mumbled under her breath as Jeremy Haskins pushed through, notebook in hand.

"What happened?"

"Why nice to see you too, Jeremy. No, how are you feeling?"

"How are you feeling? What happened?"

"Jeremy, were you on the police scanner again?" Rose beetled her eyebrows, her expression disapproving.

"Hey, a guy's got to make a living." His watery blue eyes brightened behind his thick rimless glasses. If he hadn't been holding his notebook, Blair would have laid money he would have rubbed his hands.

"So, was it the same animal? Person? Which?" His head swung from one to the other before his gaze landed on the wide bandage on Blair's throat and stayed. "Good God, what happened?" For the first time, genuine concern in his voice.

"I got attacked by a wolf." Blair sighed.

"A wolf?" Jeremy repeated. Paper rustled as he opened his stenographer's pad and began to write.

"Be sure and mention it's black or every trigger-happy hunter in the area will be out shooting every wolf in the county, which by the way is not in season. And if man's best friend happens to be out roaming, he'll probably be in trouble too."

"Good point. Mind if I sit down?" Without waiting for an answer, he dropped into a straight back chair and continued to scribble feverishly.

"So, Rose, were you attacked by the same wolf?"

Rose and Blair shared a look. Say it was human or animal?

Rose cleared her throat. "No, my attacker was human."

"Like Opel."

Crap. We are so in trouble. Blair wore her game face while plucking at her gown beneath the sheet.

"Opel couldn't decide whether an animal or human attacked her. Sounds like a crazy with a dog." He continued to scribble while he thought out loud.

"Have you checked out Obadiah Brown? He's got a rottweiler. Those things could probably pass for a wolf in the dark, especially a black one."

Blair choked on the bagel, she'd just brought to her mouth. "That dog is twelve years old and crippled with arthritis."

Jeremy tapped the pen to his lips unphased. "Still and all, it makes sense. Have you checked for folks in the county that own big black dogs?"

"It would be quicker to look for people that don't own big black dogs," Blair said dryly. She picked up her coffee, took several gulps and sat it down.

Jeremy reached for it.

"Get your own."

"Come on, Blair. We've shared spit before."

Rose's jaw dropped.

"A kiss beneath mistletoe at the town party does not constitute sharing spit." Blair shook her head.

"A fella can dream, can't he?" He grinned at her.

"You're incorrigible."

He pushed up. "So, you are sticking to your story that it was a wolf."

"That's right."

"And you, a human even though there were scratches on your neck?"

Rose elevated her chin. "Yes."

"Could there have been a dog or wolf around?"

She shrugged. "It was dark. I can't say."

"Did you talk to old man Stone?"

"Yes, but we'll be going back." And asking him if he bred any black wolfdogs.

"Okay. I'm out of here. Rose, glad you're better. Blair, hope you are soon feeling better." He bulleted through the door, calling as it swung shut, "Check the headlines tomorrow."

"Well crap," Blair said.

"You can say that again," Rose echoed.

~*~

Mateo had just shucked his clothes and stretched out on the bed when someone pounded on the door. The pounding came again. He heaved a sigh and scooped up his pants. Sliding into them, he walked on bare feet to the door, waited for a moment and let his senses take over. He smelled the jacked-up pheromones of Jesse Kipp.

He opened the door and leaned against the frame, his stance casual, his gaze alert. "You weren't who I was expecting on the other side of the door. What's up, Kipp?"

"Have you seen Layla Sosa?"

So, she hadn't gone back to the cabin. She'd probably holed up somewhere to heal. He hoped to hell she bled out. Wishful thinking on his part. He would have hunted her today, but he could move more unobtrusively at night. Still he had no business sleeping while she was on the loose. None at all.

He pulled away from the door jamb and straightened. "Her name is Delilah Devon and she's dangerous, Jesse."

Jesse visibly tensed. "What are you talking about?"

"Your girlfriend, her name is Delilah Devon and she's dangerous."

"How the hell would you know? Have you been checking up on her?" Jesse clenched and unclenched his fists. He looked a hair's breath away from taking a swing.

"I knew her years ago. I know what she's capable of."

Jesse's face went from an alarming shade of red to white back to red again. "Have you seen her?"

Not in human form. "No."

"Is she like you?"

"What are you talking about?"

Jesse snorted, wheeled and trotted off the porch. "I know what you are."

Mateo tensed. "And what am I?"

Jesse didn't bother to answer, just got in his cruiser and drove away.

Mateo stared after the cruiser. Twice now Jesse had alluded to a knowledge that Mateo hoped to hell he didn't possess. A chill crawled down his spine. And if he did, what would he do with it?

CHAPTER 16

Well hell.

If Kipp did know anything, there wasn't a damn thing he could do about it. He might as well get dressed and get to Grizzly. He'd swing by the hospital then check on some of the more remote areas of the county. Though, his gut told him Delilah was on the reservation. No doubt holed up in a remote part of the mountains.

He showered, dressed and drove to the Bean, picked up two large coffees and headed for the hospital. The doctor came through Blair's door before Mateo could go in.

"How is she, Doc?"

"Better. Much better." He kept walking. "Sorry, I got a baby to deliver. I told Blair it was your fault she has to spend another night."

"Coward," Mateo called after him.

Greene put his thumb in the air in acknowledgement.

Mateo managed to open the door with a forefinger and his foot then push his way in.

Rose got to her feet.

"Rose, I should have brought you a cup."

"Thanks, but I'm heading to the jail."

Blair glared at him. "You told him to keep me here?"

"You're on your own." Rose slipped out the door.

Fire sparked in Delaney's eyes. He came close to patting his chest for flying embers.

"It's for your own good." He put a cup on her bedside tray before he noticed the empty. He shrugged. Delaney could drink coffee straight from the pot.

"Do you have any idea how much I loathe that phrase?"

His shoulders rose then dropped.

"I can and will check myself out."

She shot her legs over the side of the bed, ready to hop out. Remembering her hospital gown, she grabbed the back.

"If you do, I'll insist you take two-weeks sick leave before returning to work."

"You can't do that!" Indignation simmered just below the surface. She looked like a volcano ready to blow. He wondered what riding all that pent-up passion would be like before he curbed his unruly thoughts.

He took a step forward, entering her space. "I can and will. I'm the sheriff remember? I can do any damn thing I please." It was hardly the most conciliatory thing to say, but frustration rolled out with the words, on so many levels. His inability to find Delilah, his unwilling attraction to Blair. Still, he should have kept it in check.

"I can't believe you said that."

Time to give conciliatory a try. "Come on, Blair. It's only one night." Frustration fought its way to the surface along with his wolf. He growled. "That bitch nearly ripped your throat out."

"Did you just growl?"

He started, then forced all expression from his face except boredom.

She sniffed. "And you smell wolfie."

"Wolfie?" His left eyebrow shot up.

"Whenever you get stressed or frustrated or plain ole pissed, you get this spicy, animal tang."

Damn her. She missed very little. "So, what you're telling me is my soap and deodorant don't hold up?"

The tension thick as storm air evaporated, rolling out as quickly as it had rolled in. They both snapped the tops of their coffee lids at the same time and took a swig.

"So, you think the wolf is a female?"

"As much trouble as this thing is, I'd have to say yes."

"Geez, Grey, can you get anymore sexist?"

He shrugged.

Her fingers drummed against the bedrail.

"You probably don't need any more caffeine."

She shrugged. "What I need is this IV out."

The IV on the hand of the drumming fingers.

"Want me to check with Pearl?"

Before she could respond, Pearl came sailing in. "Looks like that IV is coming out."

"Thank Christ."

"Watch your language, young lady." Pearl frowned.

Mateo bit back a grin. "Guess I'll be heading to the jail. We got a deal?"

"Yeah." She waved a dismissive hand at him.

"See you later then."

Carrying his coffee in one hand, he rubbed his forehead with the other. Delaney as his Chief Deputy was both a blessing and a curse. And right at this moment there was no doubt in his mind, which camp she fell in.

~*~

In spite of the caffeine flowing through her system, Blair managed to sleep on and off all day. After the influx of visitors in the morning, the rest of the day had been strangely quiet. She probably would have slept straight through the day if Pearl hadn't come in periodically to poke, prod and take her blood. And what the hell was that about? Hadn't she damn well lost enough already? Just thinking about the hot, sticky liquid gushing from her throat made her shiver.

The door swished and Evangeline strolled in.

"Hi, Evangeline. Changing of the guard?"

"Yes, ma'am."

With cool fingers, the nurse picked up her wrist and took her pulse. When she finished, she nodded with a satisfied gleam.

"Jerome behaving himself?"

Evangeline gave a throaty chuckle. "Ever since you put the fear of God in him."

"He told you about that?" That jolted her.

"No, but word gets around." She laughed again. "Thanks. You made my life easier."

"You were doing fine on your own. That young man is smart as a whip. He'll probably make a great politician."

"Lord save us." She threw her hands up. "I've got no use for politicians."

"I know what you mean." She thought of smarmy Alistair trying to take Mateo's job. If the unbelievable happened, she'd pack her bags and move back to Atlanta before she'd work for that slimy snake. She'd managed to put off their 'date' with one excuse after another and had every intention of continuing to.

Evangeline patted her hand. "Try to get some sleep. I'll be back around midnight."

Great. She forced a sickly smile and nodded.

Not that she was willing to admit it, but the attack and blood loss had left her weaker than she liked. If you discounted the poking and prodding, the extra night in the hospital gave her the chance to rest. Without much trouble she fell back to sleep.

She barely surfaced when Evangeline came in at midnight and quietly left.

She dreamed of lightning and thunder and hail bouncing off a metal roof. The thunder and lightning subsided but the hail didn't. Then it changed. She was a little girl again, playing with chalk on a blackboard. The chalk had a mind of its own and kept making scraping sounds even when she put it down.

Only it wasn't chalk.

She surfaced. The scratching came again. An eerie, grating sound. Holy crap. Someone was scratching against the ground level window. It faced the back of the building with nothing but prairie grass and trees behind it.

She scooted off the bed, bulleted to her locker and grabbed the Glock at the bottom of her clothes. She left the lights off and crept to the window. Her heart thundering, she threw back the curtains.

Green eyes, rimmed with red, stared back at her. A tongue lolled out of the creature's mouth, white fangs visible. She'd swear it smirked at her. Blair raised her gun balancing it with one hand under the other, prepared to fire. Then shook herself. Dammit, she couldn't fire through a hospital window.

She raced out of the room, heading for the exit just past the nursing station. That thing wasn't getting away this time.

"Blair, where are you going?" Evangeline yelled from behind the counter.

Blair bulleted for the door, not stopping. It wasn't going to best her again.

She heard Evangeline's frantic voice on the phone, "Sheriff, Blair is racing for the exit, she's got a police revolver in one hand and wearing nothing but that hospital gown with her hinnie hanging out.

"But, Sheriff—"

She hoped to hell he'd told her to stay put. In the distance a siren sounded. He must have been nearby. Then all thoughts of Mateo and Evangeline disappeared as she threw open the door and faced the wolf.

The hair on the back of her neck stood up. In the dark, only glowing green eyes were visible. The eeriness made her heart thump and her feet stumble. Slowly, her eyes adjusted and the night sky took on gray overtones. The smell of sanitizer replaced with crisp fresh air. The cement slab cold beneath bare feet.

Stars and a full moon sharpened her vision. Though, the last thing she needed was a wolf and full moon. Not that she believed in any of that bullshit. Still....

She raised her Glock.

The wolf growled and stepped deeper into the shadows.

Blair took a couple of steps away from the weak, yellow overhead light where early-spring bugs danced and buzzed, and stopped. She'd gone as far as she was going. This time she was going to be smart about it and not be led down the garden path or, in this case, deeper into the shadows by a she-wolf from hell.

She stood waiting, heart pumping, gun aimed in front of her in a two-handed grip.

A noise came from the left. A broken branch? A thrown stone? Wolves didn't throw stones, she reminded herself. She shivered. Evil surrounded her and crept closer.

Instinct had her whirling around. A shadow? A sense of a shadow?

"Come out, you she-bitch." She was beginning to agree with Mateo, her spidey sense told her the wolf was female. She saw nothing but heard a low growl.

She aimed at the sound and fired.

A yip of pain came out of the dark.

The night swallowed her as she ran toward the sound. Then car lights blinded her. The shrill sound of a siren cut off as Mateo skidded the police cruiser to a halt inches from her and jumped out.

"Blair, you damn idiot."

"I hit it."

He reached back in and grabbed his flashlight. "Get back in the hospital or get in the cruiser." He flashed his light around the ground. "Where was it?"

She trotted toward him, pointing toward the cruiser. "Back in the trees."

"Fine. Now get back in the clinic."

"Not on your life. I'm going with you."

"Not with your ass hanging out. Now get in the hospital or wait for me in the cruiser."

Come to think of it, there was a definite cold breeze blowing along said ass. "I'll wait in the cruiser. Holler if you need me."

He snorted and disappeared in the dark, his light bobbing.

She took two running steps, leaped into the still-running SUV and cranked up the heat. She squinted, following the progress of the bobbing light till it disappeared into the black.

Pulling her gown together to ward off the chill of the leather on her hind end and the back of her thighs, she twitched around trying to get comfortable. She cracked the window just enough to hear. Still nervy from the damn wolf, she locked the doors. She'd unlock them before Mateo got back, unwilling to let him know the beast had unnerved her.

A heavy scent of cloves and animal musk hit her a second before she heard the unsuccessful click of the door handle. A crimson-painted fingernail clicked against the windshield. For a second paralysis engulfed her before she shook it off, grabbed her gun and was out of the SUV. As the wolf came around the side of the cruiser, snarling and bleeding, she hopped back in.

Determination shot through her. She raised the Glock with one hand and rolled down the window with the other. With a burst of speed, the wolf disappeared into the dark. She started to pull the trigger then sighed. Mateo was out there somewhere. If she shot him, she'd never hear the end of it.

She started to hit the horn to get Mateo's attention then stopped, her hand hovering over the horn. Even Mateo couldn't catch that she-devil now. Instead, she rummaged through Mateo's glove compartment, found a chocolate bar, unwrapped it, munched and settled in to wait.

It wasn't long before he came trudging back, his light waving in front of him. The interior light came on as he opened the door. He glanced at her. "You ate my chocolate bar."

"How—"

He reached over and ran his thumb over the corner of her mouth then licked his digit. Blair's pulse picked up and her eyes glazed.

He climbed into the cruiser. "I didn't see a sign

of it. A spattering of blood here and there that disappeared."

She cleared her throat and licked dry lips. "It was here."

His head whipped around. "What?"

No way was she going to mention the white hand and red nails. As far as she was concerned it was a hallucination. Just like Rose's and Opel's. What in sweet hell was going on? It had to be a serial attacker and a wolf-dog. It had to be.

"Before I could get a shot off it disappeared into the woods."

Cursing low, but fluently, he threw the cruiser in gear, turned around and got back on the dim lit road.

Blair perked up. "Are you breaking me out?"

"I'm taking you to my place."

She batted her eyelashes and said in an exaggerated southern drawl, "Why I declare, Sheriff, aren't you even going to offer me dinner first?"

He snorted. "The safest place you can be right now is with me. I never expected her to go after you at the hospital. I suppose I should have."

"What the hell are you talking about?" Her brow corrugated. She shook her head, bewildered.

"Never mind."

Too tired to push it, she leaned her head against soft leather and closed her eyes. "Just take me home."

"Sorry, Delaney, but till things settle down you're staying with me."

She shifted and smooth leather rubbed bare ass. "I need to go home and get clothes."

"Got a duffle with your clothes in the back." He slowed as his headlights shone on a stray yellow cat trotting across the road.

That roused her. She blinked her eyes open and straightened. "How—. Rose. She must have a key to every house in the county. Yours excluded."

He shrugged. "I don't lock up."

She shook her head and muttered, "I'll never get used to that."

"You can take the girl out of the city but you can't take the city out of the girl." He grinned.

"Very wise," she mumbled, slumping back into the seat.

"Delaney, we're here."

"What?" She must have dozed off. She pushed at the edge of the bandage on her neck. The sutures pinched and the wound burned. She just wanted to slip back into a deep dark sleep beneath pain and fear.

"We're here."

"Umm."

The bench seat did a soft groan and the car door slammed. She should get up. She could always crawl inside, she thought muzzily.

The side door opened. Strong arms lifted her out. "Put me down, you'll throw your back out."

"You are heavier than you look," he teased, getting a better hold and scooping her up against his chest.

She decided to ignore the remark about her weight and snuggled in. The heat of him offset the chilly wind that burrowed under her night gown and bit at bare skin. For just this once, she'd let feminism go by the wayside.

Owls hooted and a few hardy male crickets chirped as they crossed the yard. Mateo's boot heels clicked across the porch. He opened the door and blessed warmth encompassed her. A few moments later he was laying her on a bed that smelled of outdoors and pine. He rolled her to the side, pulled back the sheets, lifted her again and tucked her in. "Sleep well, Delaney."

"Mmm." A butterfly light touch trailed down her cheek as she tumbled deep into sleep. The last sound she heard, a low mournful howl.

~*~

The smell of coffee woke her. She lifted her nose, sniffed, stretched and crawled out of bed. She hadn't paid attention to her surroundings last night. She didn't think Mateo had even turned on the light, just dumped her into bed like a sale item tumbled out of the bag after a day spent shopping.

She looked around. Like the rest of the house it was utilitarian. Honey-colored, knotty pine paneling glowed from spacious walls in contrast to the plain white walls of her tiny bedroom. No curtains interfered with the view. A simple pine dresser and a wide bed were the room's only furnishings. If nothing else they had minimalism in common. Maybe it was a cop thing.

Her large black duffle sat on the floor beside her legs, its sides bulging. She bent to pick it up and a wave of dizziness hit her. Okay, not back to normal, but better. Definitely, better. Once the room quit spinning, she ruffled through the bag and found her uniform and boots. She'd broke down and bought western boots last year with a yellow hand tooled rose in the center of each shaft. If Mateo saw those roses, she'd never hear the end of it. Southern belles in the West, etc. etc.

She pulled out a tan blouse and pants, and dressed. Bless Rose for putting them in the duffle instead of purposely leaving them out. Rose knew Blair would go back to work come hell or high water. She ran a thick heavy black belt through her pants loops then stomped into her boots.

Rose had even packed her toothbrush and hairbrush. Except for lip balm she seldom wore makeup, so she wasn't surprised not to find any in the duffle. Not wearing makeup, except on specific occasions, was another cause of distress for her mother. The thought made her grin. Picking up her toiletries, she made her way to the hall bathroom.

Minutes later, she followed her nose to the kitchen. To her surprise the sheriff had bacon and eggs going. He looked up from sputtering grease to give her a slow assessing once-over, lingering on racoon-ringed eyes before returning his attention to the skillets.

"Do you fix this every morning?" She walked to the coffeemaker and poured dark, rich-looking liquid into a turquoise-colored mug sitting on the black granite countertop beside the coffeemaker.

The first sip hit her belly and kicked in. She sighed

with pleasure.

"Nope. Figured you'd need it."

"You got that right." Her stomach growled as she plopped onto a chair at a pine table the same color as her bedroom walls. She ran her hand along its smooth surface. "Nice table."

"I made it."

"Well, aren't you the man of varied and hidden talents." Impressed in spite of herself she was determined not to show it. She didn't want him to think she was one of his swooning groupies.

With an economy of movement, he scooped up eggs, bacon and pulled toast out of the toaster, divided them on two plates and placed one in front of her.

He dropped down on the bench on the other side of the table and watched as she took a cautious bite and swallowed.

"Not bad, Grey."

He grinned as she dug in.

They ate in silence.

"You know you could take another day off. You're still pretty pasty." He scooped up their plates and rinsed them off in the sink.

She rolled her eyes. "You sure know how to sweet talk a girl, Sheriff."

"You're not a girl, you're my chief deputy."

Since she couldn't figure out if she'd been praised or dissed, she said nothing.

"Let's go." He shut off the water and headed for the door.

"Wait. You got a to-go-mug?"

"Pot's empty. We'll stop at the Bean."

CHAPTER 17

The din of voices clamored at him, hurting his ears as he and Delaney strode into the jailhouse. Or more accurate, he strode. Delaney swaggered.

"Sheriff," Quinn yelled covering the mouthpiece of the radio, then in a slightly lower voice, "Glad you're back, Blair."

"Good to see you, Blair. Sign these would you, Sheriff." Adam waved a stack of papers.

"Hospital's on the line, Sheriff. Wants to know if you kidnapped Blair," Rose called with her hand over the speaker. Squawking still managed to escape through her fingers. "Oh, hi, Blair." Rose grinned.

"Quinn, take a message.

"Rose, tell the hospital Delaney will be by sometime today to sign herself out.

"Adam, give me those papers."

Adam shoved the stack of papers at him, along with a copy of *The Grizzly*. "You better see this, Boss. How are you, Blair?"

The headlines screamed WOLFMAN OR FIEND WHO OWNS A DANGEROUS WOLFDOG?

"Well, shit." He scanned the paper. Opel had given a brief statement. Rose even briefer.

Quinn had a stack of note pads that he waved as soon as he got off the radio. "Dozens of sightings, Mateo. Everything from red glowing eyes to horns. Though, half the callers were at the bar last night while I was playing, weren't they, Rose?"

As a man, so to speak, they turned to stare at Rose. She blushed. "What? I drank soda."

"I think it's great you went to hear Quinn, Rose," Delaney said.

Rose DeWitt in a bar, was the world ending? Wouldn't surprise him a bit as crazy as things were getting.

Before he could escape, the door opened.

"Well, Alistair Etheridge as I live and breathe," Blair drawled.

He rushed to her side and put his hands on her shoulders and gently squeezed. Her gaze lasered first one hand then the other till he dropped them. "I heard you'd been hurt. I stopped by the clinic this morning but they said you'd already left, by questionable means." He glanced at Mateo and smirked.

Mateo fought down hackles that had a tendency to rise. He didn't smile. The guy was good-looking in a soft, well-tended, rich sort of way. "What brings you here, Etheridge?"

Alistair arranged his face till it showed solemn concern. Unfortunately, he couldn't hide the gleam in his eyes.

"Have you seen this?" He held a copy of *The Grizzly.*

No doubt about it, the shark smelled blood in the water and was circling.

Mateo lifted his copy.

"What are you going to do to protect the citizens of this fair county?"

Fair county? "Drop the affronted act, you don't have any votes here."

"You never know." He gave a confident smile that swept the occupants in the room.

Blair rolled her eyes and Rose frowned. Adam flushed. Why was anybody's guess.

"You don't have mine." Adam lifted his chin.

Mateo's lips twitched. Anger accounted for the red in the young man's face.

"Are you even old enough to vote?" Etheridge asked rudely.

"He is and so are the rest of us," Quinn growled. "You're wasting your time here."

"Appreciate the backing. I'll take you all to the polls in the cruiser on election day." Mateo stuck his papers on Adam's desk, put his hands in his pockets and rocked on his heels. A grin on his face.

Etheridge's face turned an ugly shade of puce. "You haven't answered my question, Sheriff, what do you intend to do about this?"

He slammed the paper on Rose's desk, hard enough to make her jump.

A hard look in his eyes, Quinn started to rise.

Mateo waved him back. "I intend to bring whoever is responsible for this to justice." His eyes lighted briefly on Rose then Blair. Delilah would pay.

At the expression on his face, Blair's eyes widened.

"See that you do." Alistair shoved out the door,

slamming it behind him.

"That one's going to be trouble." Quinn thrummed his fingers on the desk.

"We'll cross that bridge when we come to it. Blair go to the hospital and check yourself out. Adam, you go with her and make sure she goes and comes straight back."

"Yes, sir." He looked both elated and frightened. Blair would tear a strip out of him, in a delightful southern way of course, if he crossed her.

"Really?" She fisted her hands on her hips.

"Sooner you go, the sooner you'll get back." He headed for the office before she could argue.

As he closed the door, he heard Delaney. "Come on, Adam. Maybe that cute girl you like is volunteering today."

Mateo grinned. He took a sip of his rapidly cooling coffee then got down to paperwork.

The plain wall clock's hands were inching toward noon by the time he finished making calls, calming people down and signing paperwork.

A knock sounded and Rose walked in carrying a cup and paper bag. He sniffed. Ham. Coffee. His stomach growled.

"Forget Quinn and marry me, Rose." He put his hand on his heart then reached for the bag she'd nearly dropped at his words.

"They say the way to a man's heart is through his stomach." She laughed then added belatedly. "Quinn and I are just friends."

Mateo wisely stayed silent on the subject. He lifted

his bag. "Thanks for this."

Rose's expression grew dark. Dark, at least, for someone with her cheerful personality. More like a gray-tinged, wispy cloud flitting across the sun. He wondered, yet again, how she'd managed in law enforcement all these years when one saw the worst that humanity had to give out. "Boss, Alistair is going from store to store, getting everyone stirred up. He's trying his best to cause trouble for you."

He studied her. The distress visible on her features. She still had a scratch on her cheek that hadn't quite healed. The pulse in her neck beat quicker than it should and the animal in him heard her heart thump in agitation.

"And you went behind him and calmed everyone down that he riled up, didn't you?"

"Part of my job is to check on the citizens of Grizzly." She drew herself up to her full five foot three and pushed out a rounded chin.

"They appreciate it and so do I. Thanks, Rose. You're the glue that holds this department together."

"You hold us together, Boss." She smiled and left the office.

"I never can get the last word in with the women in this office." He shook his head but a smile lurked on his lips as he pulled out his sandwich.

~*~

Overall, the day passed smoothly with less uproar over the paper's headlines than he'd expected. He credited Rose for that.

"Are you ready, Delaney?"

"Yeah. Let me make one call then you can drop me at my house." She tossed it out like a gauntlet thrown down.

"Do you want to fill out your paperwork for sick leave now then?"

She glared at him.

He only smiled and strode to Quinn. "Are you still staying with Rose?"

"She's kindly putting me up while my apartment is being fumigated, painted and some remodeling done." Quinn grinned.

"Hope you don't have to burn it down." Mateo modulated his voice so that only Quinn heard him.

"You and me both. What about Blair?" Quinn lowered his raspy voice too.

"She'll be staying with me till this matter is settled."

Quinn nodded his approval. "See you tomorrow."

"Tomorrow." He watched Delaney thump down the phone and stomp out the door, liking the way her uniform fit snug across her hips.

He strode after her, hopped in the SUV and started the engine. "Think of it as going undercover."

"I beg your pardon?" Her jaw dropped.

He pulled out and headed down Main Street.

"Have you ever thought that it's not about protecting you but about drawing out whomever you managed to piss off, so I can catch them?"

The engine idled as he stopped at one of the few stoplights in town.

"You're using me for bait."

He could almost hear the wheels turning as she mulled this over.

"So, you're not just doing this to protect me?"

He could have sworn disappointment flashed across her face. He almost threw his hands up. Was there any understanding women? She was pissed if she thought he was protecting her and disappointed if she thought he wasn't.

"Yes. You draw her out, I'll nail her." His hands tightened on the wheel in anticipation of bringing down Delilah.

"So, we are no longer talking in euphemistic terms about your ex but back to referring to *her*?"

He dug deep for patience. "My gut tells me its Delilah but I have no proof." His foot hit the gas as they left Grizzly behind.

"If it is, I may have pissed her off, but it's you she wants to get back at."

"I know." His hands tightened again before he forced himself to relax. He needed a good run.

They turned onto his long, winding lane. When the house came into view, Blair jerked forward in her seat. "Why are wolves sitting on your porch?"

CHAPTER 18

Mateo's pulse beat in his throat. The old wolf and the pup always waited at the edge of the clearing. Why in hell were they on the porch?

"Wait here." He killed the engine and leaped for the porch.

The pup whimpered. His shoulder torn open. Reddish-brown splotches of blood stained the light-wooden floor around him.

"Damn her." He swore fiercely. Rage rushed through him. He fought down the wolf who yearned to turn, find Delilah and rip her throat out. The pup had almost healed from the trap. It had gained in weight, size and confidence. The damn evil woman had gone and ruined all that.

The cruiser's door opened and closed. The old wolf moved off the porch, as Blair came rushing up, but stayed close by.

Mateo picked the pup up and carried it inside.

"What happened?"

The pup cowered against him as Blair got close.

"Something tore him up." He moved inside the house.

"You think it was Delilah's wolfdog?"

"In a sense."

"In a sense?"

He redirected the subject. "It looks a lot like your neck. Lucky for the little one, it's his shoulder and no arteries are involved."

Blair winced and touched her bandage as she looked at the flapping, bloody skin from a triangular tear.

"What are you going to do?"

"Sew him up."

"Will he let you?" Her expression skeptical.

"I'll spray an antiseptic topical pain killer on it. Get the door will ya?"

She hurried forward and opened the unlocked door. "Of course," she muttered.

"What's that?" He grinned. He'd heard her perfectly.

"Nothing."

He looked at the wolf. "You coming in?"

The animal plopped his furry butt on the grass in front of the porch, his tongue hanging out. As if he understood every word, Blair thought.

They trooped inside. Mateo hung a right. He cradled the pup in one hand and opened the door with the other. To look at them, it looked like any man holding his dog. Only it wasn't a dog but a wild wolf, perfectly at home in Mateo's arms. The hair on the back of her arms rose. It was a bit too woo-woo.

She shook herself. Babies were babies, no matter what the species. This pup was no different.

She followed him into a room, with requisite honey-colored paneling, that she'd never been in before. An all-purpose table, with a crème colored granite countertop, stood between a huge mahogany desk and a comfortable, worn leather couch. Books spilled out of a wooden bookcase that ran from floor to ceiling. The room's neutrality broken by a bright red and violent black zigzag throw rug.

"What can I do?"

"Get the medical kit. It's in the towel closet off the main bathroom."

"I'll be right back."

She bulleted to the bathroom and opened the closet. A large medical kit sat next to a stack of deep blue towels. She grabbed it, along with one of the towels and a bottle of hand sanitizer and trotted down the hall.

He still held the pup, stroking it. He nodded toward the table. The supplies landed with a soft thud as she dropped them on the clean surface.

"There's thread in there and a needle. Would you thread the needle for me?"

She pulled out a needle shaped like a half circle. "This?"

"That's right."

"Where did you get it?"

"My dad was a medic."

"Oh yeah. I heard he's living the good life in Puerto Rico."

He grunted.

She closed one eye, squinted and threaded it.

"Great. Now hand me that antiseptic spray."

She passed it to him.

The pup wriggled as he sprayed the wound. "Little cold is it?"

He put the can down and reached for the needle.

"You want me to hold him?"

"Yeah."

"He won't bite me, will he?"

"Well if he does it won't be as bad as the last bites."

She grimaced and gingerly took the pup. The little wolf didn't seem to be any happier about the situation than she was.

Mateo spoke low to the pup and began to sew. The pup whimpered occasionally but overall stayed quiet. Mateo worked quickly. In no time, he'd finished.

"Hey you're pretty good with a needle. If I bring you a pattern and material will you make me a prom dress?"

He snorted. "Har de har. I'm going to take a walk around the property. Make yourself at home."

"Mind if I come?"

"Nope. I don't mind."

He scooped up the pup and headed for the porch.

"You think he'll be safe out there?"

"As long as he stays with the old one. I'm assuming he wandered off or she would never have gotten him."

Again, he'd used the word she. Well, Blair didn't disagree with him. She was pretty sure it was Delilah and a wolfdog she'd trained to kill. Nothing was going to give her more pleasure than hauling Delilah's sorry ass to jail. She touched her bandaged neck. It was beginning to itch. A sure sign it was healing.

The old wolf came trotting from the trees. She got a good look at him and gave a start. Out of the corner of her eye she glanced at Mateo. The eye color the same. Even the shape, which on a wolf looked normal, on Mateo startling.

"What are you staring at, Delaney?"

Damn, the man had the eyes of a cat.

She pointed to the sun at his back as it dropped into the trees in the western sky. Not quite sunset, the golden orb shone through the forest, bringing out the dark bark of oak—their leaves trying to bud—making it stark and spectacular. Outlining pine needles, turning them a bright sundrenched green. "I can see why you chose this place, it's quite lovely."

"I can't take any credit for it. My father bought it and built the cabin."

The old wolf whoofed.

Mateo grinned.

"Seems he agrees with you."

"Seems he does." He set the pup on its feet and it limped to the old wolf.

The wolf turned and trotted north, the pup at his heels.

Mateo followed.

Once or twice, she tried to make conversation, but his answers were so terse she dropped any attempt. After all, she'd invited herself along.

They strode for half an hour till the wolf stopped and the sun set. Mateo continued.

"Why did the wolf stop?" She broke the silence.

"It's where my property ends."

"And you think he knows that?" She scoffed. A pinecone crunched beneath her boot as she lengthened her stride.

"He knows enough not to scare off all the wildlife in the vicinity when he's tracking."

A few steps behind him, she stuck her tongue out at him.

"Real mature, Delaney."

How did he do that?

He went a few yards farther and stopped. He turned in a slow circle, his eyes closed, his nose in the air.

She watched fascinated.

"Damn it. She's using a scent blocker." He hit his fist against his palm, frustration on his handsome features.

"How do you know that?"

"Because I can't smell her anymore."

"And you could before?" She lifted her nose and sniffed. Other than pine, she smelled nothing.

"Yes. I have a very well-developed olfactory. I smelled her that night at Caulfield's but it was hidden in a man's leather jacket, men's cologne and wolf."

"You smelled all that?"

"Think back. What did you smell?"

"Blood," she answered flatly.

"That too, but didn't you smell anything else?"

She closed her eyes, and concentrated hard, trying to remember an elusive scent. Her eyes popped open and her pulse began to race. "Cologne. Jesse's cologne.

At the Caulfield's and when I was attacked." Layla/ Delilah would have access to it. Proof of a sort. Though, nothing that would stand up in court. She was surprised Mateo hadn't zoomed in on it, considering how he'd zeroed in on every other scent, but then maybe not. She'd only noticed it on Jesse once or twice and both times he'd been off duty. Apparently, he didn't want his bad-ass Chief of Police image damaged by something as frivolous as cologne. It was a distinctive woodsy scent. She'd asked him about it and he told her one of the women had made it specifically for him on his last birthday.

"It's got to be Layla. Delilah." They said at the same time.

"Let's go talk to Kipp." Mateo was already backtracking toward the cruiser.

Arms pumping, Blair trotted to catch up.

He'd already started the motor as she hopped in and was turning around in the drive before she had her seat belt fastened.

"Let me do the talking."

He didn't respond.

"He'll talk to me quicker than he will you."

"Fine. But it's only because he likes to look at you."

"No, it's because he doesn't like to look at you." She chortled and slapped her leg.

"You have a strange sense of humor, Southern girl."

She tried to think of something snappy that she could end with Western boy but when nothing came to mind she shrugged, kicked back her seat and crossed her legs then closed her eyes.

Before she knew it, Mateo was shaking her shoulder. "Wake up, Delaney."

"Damn. I drop off like an old woman." The car leather gave a soft groan as she stretched.

"You need rest. You came back to work too early."

"You're like a dog with a bone. You get an idea in your head and won't let go."

"Only when I'm right."

"Which by your calculations is all the time."

He turned off the motor. "There's a light on, looks like Kipp is home." They'd parked in front of a small, tan-sided house with brown shingles, on the edge of town. Similar sized houses sat on the road beside it. Unlike Mateo's, no trees were near, only brown prairie grass trying to green up.

They got out of the car, slamming the doors. As they walked up the sidewalk a bright moon trailed across a hazy, charcoal sky and hovered behind the little house, haloing it, before it continued its journey among misty clouds, the little house returning to a dull monotone.

Jesse stepped out on the porch, holding a long-neck in his hand. He flipped on the porch light as the moonlight died. "What are you doing on my property, Sheriff?"

"Is it a problem, Kipp?"

"It could be."

Men. Enough testosterone billowed around to choke an innocent bystander, in this case her. Blair rolled her eyes. She stepped past Mateo. "Can we come in, Jesse?"

"How are you, Blair?" His harsh features softened.

Three clipped steps forward and she was on his small porch. He touched the bandage on her neck. "I'm sorry to hear you got hurt."

"Mateo showed up before I got my throat ripped out."

"Was it a wolf?"

"Or a wolfdog. Have you seen Layla lately?"

"Not since you were injured."

"Can we talk?"

Jesse opened the door and motioned Blair in. He stepped in behind her and started to shut the door. Mateo, now on the porch, stuck his foot in.

"Fine." Jesse sighed and let him in. The house had an open structure, living room on the right with a short half rail that divided a small kitchen and dining room from the rest of the room.

"Want a beer?"

"Can't. I'm driving." Mateo stuck his hands in his pockets and rocked on his heels.

"I'm not. I'll take one." She stepped next to Mateo and smelled the musky scent of him that he gave off when he was under stress. Not that you'd know by looking at him.

"Do you have any idea where Layla is?"

"No. Unless something happened to her, which I'm not ruling out, I've been dumped. Why the interest? Has Grey narrowed the attacks down to Layla, since she's a newcomer?" He gave a skeptical raise of his eyebrows as he strode to the small kitchen with white cabinets and not very much counter space. He rummaged in an old refrigerator, his head in, his elbow on the door. Definitely a nice view. He had a compact build with a small, tight butt.

Mateo's eyes bore into her.

She gave him the most innocent expression she could muster.

Jesse popped the bottle cap and put the cold beverage in her hand. She raised it to him and took a deep swallow, feeling immediately better.

"Does Layla have a dog?"

Jesse who'd been about to take a swig, stopped, his hand in midair. He looked first at her then Mateo. His gaze lingering longest on the sheriff. Finally, he turned back to Blair. "Dogs don't care for Layla or she them. Why?"

"My theory is that whoever is behind the attacks has a wolfdog that she's taught to savage people and animals at her command."

Jesse's gaze swiveled back to Mateo and asked, "Is it your theory too?"

Blair's eyes narrowed. Oddly enough, the Chief didn't dismiss her theory out of hand. The question was why?

"Close enough." Mateo's features expressionless.

Her blood pressure rose and stuck in her gorge. "Damn it to hell, Mateo, I wish you'd tell me what you are being so tight-lipped about. You never entirely commit to this. What does close enough mean?"

"It means that it's a damn good theory that I'm not ruling out, but as yet we don't have proof."

Way to cover your ass. She almost voiced her thoughts but had enough sense of self-preservation to swallow the words. Instead she turned back to Jesse. "Is there any way she could have an attack dog stashed away somewhere and you not know about it?"

"Contrary to popular opinion, I keep a close ear to the ground. There's little goes on around here I don't know about." Again, his gaze rested on Mateo, a challenge in them.

Blair put a finger between her eyebrows and rubbed at the building pressure. There was some serious animosity going on between these two. Maybe coming here hadn't been such a great idea.

Holding eye contact with Jesse, Mateo said, "Tell him about the scent."

Jesse turned on his heel, his back squarely to Mateo. "What scent?"

"When I was attacked I smelled your cologne."

The chief of police's jaw dropped and his eyebrows soared. He stared at her till she got twitchy. "You think I attacked you?"

"No! Of course not. But Layla would have access to it."

"So would the woman who made it, but considering she's seventy, walks with a cane and her eyesight is failing, I think she can safely be ruled out."

"Would you let us know if you do see her? At the very least, she's a person of interest." Mateo drummed fingers on thighs.

"And if you find her?"

There it was again that tension thrumming just

below the surface as if they shared a secret she wasn't part of. She glanced from one to the other uneasily.

"Bring her to justice."

Neither broke eye contact.

"Yours or the law's?"

The conversation besides being oblique had just taken a turn to the dark.

Enough was enough. Blair took another guzzle then thumped her bottle on the tan and black granite speckled counter. "Let's go, Mateo. Thanks, Jesse. Give me a call if you find anything."

Once back in the SUV, she demanded, "What was that about?"

"What?"

"You know damn well what. The reference to vigilante justice. You're a straight arrow where the law is concerned and to the best of my knowledge so is Jesse Kipp."

Mateo turned the engine over and put on the lights. Storm clouds had rolled in and a streak of lightning speared the ground in the distance.

The shriek of an owl had goose bumps lifting on Blair's arms.

Mateo stared into the black then pulled out. "Jesse's mind is like a maze. It has a lot of twists and turns. I have no idea what's going on. But one thing I do know. He knows something that he's not sharing. I've got a feeling when he does, all hell is going to break loose."

CHAPTER 19

She had to go home, and soon, regardless of what Mateo threatened.

For three days now, she'd been at his cabin. Grizzly was a small town and he was up for re-election. Knowing Alistair, he'd find some way to work it to his advantage.

She'd fallen into the rhythm of the place, of Mateo. Gotten used to the old and young wolf that hung around. Even though they both lived in cabins in the country, hers was a rental, his a home steeped in strength and serenity. Did a building take on the characteristics of its owner? Somehow suck that energy in and make it its own? She shook her head at her whimsy. Embarrassed by it. She padded on bare feet to the pantry, stuck her head in, pulled out two russet potatoes and washed them.

Mateo strode in and leaned against the doorframe. Filling it as only a virile, good-looking male could do. He was such a sensual creature.

"You sure you want to fix dinner?"

She got her wayward thoughts back on track. "Don't look so worried. Even I, the Queen of Carryout, can fix baked potatoes, fry up steaks and toss a salad."

"If you say so."

"Do you want to fix it?" She stood with hands on hips, her eyes narrowed.

"Nope, I'd run into town and get take out."

She gave a dismissive wave.

"How long?"

"Why? Are you hungry?"

"I wanted to check the parameters of the property and need to know when to be back."

My, don't we sound domestic. The thought had her scurrying to the refrigerator and reaching for the wine bottle. "Gonna check forty acres in an hour and a half? Good luck with that."

He chuckled. A rich throaty sound that always gave her a zing in the belly. "Maybe not the whole thing. I'll be back." He strode out of the kitchen. Moments later the door thumped behind him.

Wine glass in hand, she walked to the window and watched him. The sun shone through oak and pine, hitting the silver that slicked his thick black hair and making it shine. The old wolf and the pup stood at the edge of the woods waiting for him. As soon as the pup saw him, he bounced forward frolicking around him. Mateo bent and ruffled the gray fur, sending the pup into ecstasy. The old wolf stood waiting, wagging his plumy tail, his tongue hanging out. He bumped against Mateo's leg and Mateo ran a hand down his head. Then they disappeared into the forest.

Her jaw dropped and her wine sloshed as her nerveless fingers opened. She got control of her nervous system and tightened her fingers around the stem. The young wolf, she could understand. He'd probably imprinted on Mateo. But the old wolf? A thought had her brightening. Maybe that's why he had such an animal smell to him sometimes. The scent of the old wolf on his skin.

Having settled one niggling question to her satisfaction, while raising another, she glanced at the kitchen clock, inlaid with real turquoise. Four-thirty. Perfect. Dinner at six.

~*~

She threw down the dog-eared thriller she'd been reading, thrummed fingers on her thighs and looked at her watch again. Seven o'clock. Where the hell was Mateo? He'd been gone for two and a half hours. Tension built between her shoulder blades. Something wasn't right. She grabbed her boots lying beside the black leather sofa and stomped into them. She went in the bedroom got her revolver and holster, and fastened it on. Turned the oven from low to off and strode out the door.

On the porch, she took a long look at lengthening shadows, unsure where to start. At the edge of the trees, the old wolf emerged. It gave a low whoof and stood waving its tail.

She took a few cautious steps in the wolf's direction. The gray fur that blended so perfectly with its environment disappeared in the trees. She stopped. Should she go any further? The wolf reappeared, waiting.

What the hell? She gave a mental shrug and

plunged into the dark coolness of the forest. The wolf took off at a trot. Pumping her arms, she did the same. Dry leaves crunched under her boots as the shadows lengthened. The scent of pine and loam filled the evening air. In the trees, she caught an occasional glimpse of the pup, following the old wolf but keeping a good distance from her.

She stumbled over a fallen branch she hadn't seen. Dammit, the sun was down. Why hadn't she thought to bring a flashlight?

There was no way around it. She had to go back. She wheeled and started running back, hoping she didn't trip again and twist an ankle, again.

The old wolf howled. She ignored it and kept going.

The wolf's shadow loomed as he raced beside her. Her pulse picked up and her teeth chattered. He pulled ahead and stopped in front of her making her come to a stiff-legged halt. When she moved forward, he held his ground and showed his fangs. Her hand fell on her gun butt. Her heart raced. What the hell should she do? She couldn't, wouldn't be wolf fodder again.

The wolf made no move toward her, but he wasn't letting her by either.

She took a cautious step to her left. He moved to block her.

What now?

"Dammit it. I need a flashlight. I can't see to go any further than my nose without one." She spoke out of frustration, knowing there was no way the poor dumb animal understood her.

Then a strange thing happened. The wolf moved out of the path and sat down, waiting.

The hair on the back of her neck rose. The wolf couldn't possibly understand her. This was way too woo-woo for a city girl. Cautiously, she stepped forward. The wolf sat there. When she hurried past him, he fell into step behind her. Not entirely comfortable with it, she kept her hand on her gun and kept glancing over her shoulder but he made no move to attack. The wolf gave an occasional wag of his tail. The young one whined in the underbrush.

When they reached the house, she raced across the porch, jumped in the door and slammed it behind her. She leaned against the wall with her heart pounding. "Get your big girl pants on, Delaney. Just because a dog or wolf attacked you doesn't mean this one will." She rubbed her neck that was finally beginning to heal, pushed away from the wall and strode to Mateo's closet and pulled out a flashlight.

Her shoulders thrown back, she strode out of the house and onto the porch. The old wolf waited in the thinning yellow glow of porch light that spread into the shadows.

"My what big teeth you have, Grandpa."

If wolves smiled this one did. It gave a short, huffing bark. Its tail wagged.

"You're freaking me out. Let's go."

The wolf turned and trotted into the woods in the direction they'd come.

"Move over, Alice, I'm falling down the rabbit hole." She tightened her muscles to keep her hand holding the flashlight from shaking.

Once again, the wolf gave a huffing bark as if he were laughing and wagged his tail.

Blair bit her lips together to keep any other inane remarks from escaping in case the wolf reacted again and she ran screaming down the road like a crazy thing.

They continued on for a good half an hour. Blair following the wolf, waving her flashlight in front of her. She didn't see the small animal warren till she put her left foot in it and landed face first in pine needles. "Dammit. Dammit. Dammit." Why was she such a klutz? And Mateo accused her of being a Southern belle. She snorted. Right. No matter how many dance classes her long-suffering mother had signed her up for, grace had never been her specialty. She got on her hands and knees. The wolf pup who'd grown curious came to investigate. He got within a foot of her then raced back into the shadows. She pushed to her feet.

The old wolf howled, agitated. Without waiting for her, it pushed deeper into the forest. She followed. It stopped at the two-lane road that Mateo's property bumped up against.

She flashed her light around. Shiny metal shown at the old wolf's feet. She raced forward, Mateo's clothes plunked in a pile on the ground, along with his boots and gun. Her breath hitched then came quick and light. It didn't make sense. Had someone taken him hostage?

She looked at the wolf. He'd gotten her this far. He made no move, just stared at her with those eyes that so resembled Mateo's. He turned his unwavering gaze and fixed on a spot across the road.

She waited but he made no move to leave. Mateo had once mentioned that he never left the property. Odd. She shrugged and trotted across the road.

She tripped. But this time on a piece of clothing not an animal's hole. She picked up a leather jacket. The cold seeped into her hand from the tanned animal hide. She flashed the light around and saw a pair of women's black jeans. Gingerly, she picked them up. Designer. Size 6. Rage rushed through her in a gush of heat that made her forget the night's chill.

Here she'd been fixing the bastard's dinner while he'd been out doing the dirty with some bimbo. She threw down the jacket and stomped on it. She turned her wrath on the wolf and shouted across the road. "This is what you dragged me out to see? Another notch in that horny bastard's belt?"

The wolf shook its head, sat down beside the road, threw his head up at the moon and howled. A mournful, eerie cry that had the hair on her arms standing on end and goose bumps forming.

Sanity returned with a thump. It was twenty degrees out and the clouds looked full enough to snow. It was too damn cold to do the naked rumba on the ground no matter how turned on. Not unless you had a hankering for frostbite on your private parts.

Slowly, she lifted the jacket and sniffed. It carried a musky female scent that Jesse's cologne had nearly buried. The smell surged forward from her subconscious.

SANDRA COX

Her hands shaking, she pulled out her cell and dialed the rez's Chief of Police. "Jesse, you need to get over here, quick."

CHAPTER 20

He'd nearly reached the north end of his property, an easy fifteen-minute jog from the cabin when the old wolf trotting beside him began to growl. The pup tucked its tail between its legs and leaned against Mateo.

The old wolf took the lead. His hand on his gun, Mateo followed, his steps quick and light. Nothing crunched beneath his boots. Cold air snapped his face making his breath fog up, his wolf blood heating him.

They'd nearly reached the road when he scented her. The old wolf's hackles went up and so did Mateo's. They ran forward, halting when they came to the road that ran next to the northern boundary of his property. The sun traveling westward behind gray clouds took that moment to pop out, full and ripe, lighting the sky in a blood-red halo. What it revealed iced his blood and chilled his bones.

Delilah stood across the road. She wore black skinny jeans and a form-fitting black leather jacket. Her body as beautiful as he remembered. It was her face that turned his blood to ice.

Against glorious black curls that fell in magnificent disarray peeped wolf ears. Her entire face had transformed into the black wolf he remembered and when she raised her arm, a paw with long claws peaked from the end of the jacket. He stood frozen, unable to look away. He'd heard of shapeshifters and powerful shamans who could hold a semi-transformation. It took years of dedicated training to master. In this case, four. Since he'd run her out of his county.

Her eyes never leaving him, she slid out of her jacket and shimmied out of her jeans. She wore nothing underneath. The sun glinted on white alabaster skin. Her combined form both fascinated and repelled. She stood proudly on display for several moments before transforming into full wolf. A beautiful animal. Sleek, black, with glittering green eyes. Smaller than he and possibly faster. And far more dangerous.

He raised his gun.

She disappeared into the shadows.

Shucking his clothes, he became the wolf.

He crossed the road at a dead run just as a truck sped around the corner. Tires squealed as the pickup swerved to miss him. Then he was across, swallowed by the dark of the forest, her cloying musky animal scent filling his nostrils till he reeked of it.

He raced forward following her trail. It twisted and turned, always heading north, back toward the rez.

Night fell.

No matter how fast he ran, he couldn't catch her. She'd always been fleet and while he was fast, she was faster. The best he did was an occasional glimpse of the back of that sleek black body. He pushed harder. This had to end here, tonight. Either the man would bring her to justice or the wolf would serve justice.

Shapeshifters had their own laws. Humans could not be allowed to know what walked among them for the good of both species. She had threatened his county. Hurt his people. Her attacks were accelerating. In either world, he knew the pattern. The next would be a kill.

He had been so enamored of her in the beginning it had blinded him to her true nature. The sex between them raw and explosive. Then he began to notice things. When they were in wolf form and hunted, how she prolonged the kills, drew pleasure on the fear and pain of the hunted.

When he killed, he killed for food and killed cleanly. What she did disgusted him. He'd been on the verge of breaking it off the day he caught her on the trail of a small child that had wandered away from her family and property. That was when he'd sent her packing. He'd gone back and reunited the child with her relieved parents. They'd never forgotten and would go to the wall for him, even though he was only doing his job. Humans were funny that way.

Sharp winds ruffled his coat and caused bare tree limbs to bend and rustle, throwing eerie shadows on the ground. He'd crossed onto the rez a few miles back.

As he followed her up the mountain, the pine grew thicker. The air thinner. More tangy. A coyote caught sight of him then slunk back into the dark. A deer took off in fright. The wind rose and howled around him as if in pain. They were heading toward the cabin.

He reached the cabin and stopped but her scent didn't. He sniffed, caught it and continued on. Winding ever upward.

His legs tired. His chest hurt from his heart pounding hard against it. He'd always been the one with the stamina. Delilah had tired easily. Not anymore.

A sharp rock sticking up through the grass pricked his front paw. The pain only pushed him on, making him more determined.

His concentrated focus on the scent cost him.

As the cliff rushed forward, he stiffened his legs, dust spurting around him. His front paws were over the ledge before he caught himself, his nails digging in, fighting for purchase. Pebbles went flying, down, down, down. One larger rock made a smashing sound when it hit bottom. Whining uneasily, he moved backward.

"I almost pushed you over, but that would have been too quick. Too easy."

He whipped around.

The moon haloed her white body. Her green eyes glittered in the dark. Some would call them cat eyes. They would be wrong. They were the eyes of a wolf.

He changed form. The wind pricked his naked skin while it whipped Delilah's hair around her head in a wanton halo. "Hello, Delilah."

"Hello, Mateo."

"I told you never to come back."

"Yet here I am. Remember this place?" She made a motion with her arms to encompass the ledge.

"Can't say as I do." He raised an eyebrow, his expression bored, while inside his pulse pounded.

She laughed. "Of course, you do, darling. We snuck onto the rez in wolf form and ran for hours. We ended on this shelf and made mad love."

"I'm not sure wolves make love, Delilah. What we had between us was more—bestial."

"Call it what you want, but it was good for us."

"Your tastes grew a little too depraved for me." He straightened, every sense alert. "So, what do you want? Why did you bring me here?"

She laughed. A gay sound tinged with madness. "Since we mated here. I thought it only fitting that you die here." Her languid pose disappeared. Fast as the rushing wind, she picked up a knife off a waist-high outcrop, she'd apparently left for this purpose, and sent it singing toward him. He threw himself to the left.

Too slow.

It missed the heart but caught his shoulder.

She changed into half-human half-beast and leaped on him. Biting. Raking him with her claws.

He hit her between the eyes knocking her back long enough for him to change back into a wolf. The change took longer, his movements sluggish from his slashed shoulder. With every movement, he hosed the ledge with his hot spurting blood.

As he crouched and gathered himself to jump, she changed too.

They met in midair, snarling, biting, clawing. His fangs bit deep into her chest. She howled and sunk hers into his throat. He managed to break her hold before they bit into an artery. Still she'd done damage.

He leaped at her and tore an ear. She managed to get her fangs into his jaw. Scratching at his hind quarters with her claws. Neither letting go, they rolled along the ledge, their only goal to end the other.

Mateo was the first to feel the dirt crumbling at the end of the ledge. He tried to push her back. But she was too far gone to her surroundings, the blood lust too strong to pay attention to anything but the kill.

They went over the edge, locked in a deadly embrace. Her paws tightened around him. For one brief moment, she turned into the beautiful woman he remembered. "I loved you in my own way." The black wolf returned and she held eye contact with his as the wind whistled and the ground rose up to meet them.

He tried to turn so that his body would hit the ground first but it was no use. His strength gone. Blood flowed like droplets of rain as they bulleted through the air.

She hit the ground. He landed hard on top of her.

CHAPTER 21

"What's up? I just ordered pizza and opened a beer. Can't you call Mateo?"

"It's about Mateo." She stood shaking in the cold, staring at the clothes at her feet. The Glock safely tucked in her belt.

"And you are calling me because?"

She ignored that and continued, trying to keep her teeth from chattering. With her free hand, she turned up her jacket collar. "He was late coming home for dinner so I went out looking for him—"

"You're calling me because he's late for dinner? Sorry, the pizza boy just pulled up, I'll call you later."

"Jesse, wait."

The line went dead.

She took a deep breath, closed her eyes and forced down impatience and rising fear. She dialed again.

"Damn it, Blair—"

"I found his clothes and gun by the side of the road."

Jesse didn't answer. The silence stretched. Finally, he spoke. "I wouldn't worry too much about it. Give him a couple of hours. He'll be home."

She frowned, unsure what she'd expected him

to say. She certainly hadn't expected such a blasé attitude about finding Mateo's clothes and gun beside the road.

"A woman's clothes were on the other side." She added it deliberately. Waiting for his response, wondering if he would make a sarcastic remark.

"Well I'll be damned. Looks like he was on the right track all along."

"Do you know something I don't?"

"Yeah, I think I do. Where are you?"

"The north side of his property."

"Facing the rez." It wasn't a question.

"That's right."

"I'll be there soon." The line went dead.

She paced. Back and forth. Back and forth. The sky cloudy. The wind piercing. She turned up her collar. The old wolf ignored her, his gaze on the road. The young pup slunk out of the woods to lie beside his pack member. The old one paid him no mind, continuing his vigil. If her restless steps got close, the pup would slink back into the woods then back out again when she moved away.

Something was wrong. Dead wrong. Her spidey sense was all over the board. She kept thinking Mateo would come bounding back and explain this craziness. But he didn't.

"Come on, Jesse." Her breath shallow, she kept pacing but found herself staring at the road, much like the old wolf.

Time dragged. Seconds minutes. Minutes hours. Or so it seemed.

Finally, she heard the wail of a siren. "It's about damn time."

The wolf barked.

"Damn straight." She nodded then threw her hands in the air. "Great. Now I'm talking to dumb animals."

The wild canine growled.

"I wish you wouldn't do that. It's like you understand everything I'm saying. It's creeping me out." Then her gaze turned to the road, the wolf forgotten as Jesse came roaring up, his siren on, his blue light flashing.

He pulled to the side of the road, jumped out of the vehicle and slammed the door.

"Show me."

She pointed to the pile of clothes beside the road.

"And the other."

"Over here." She trotted across the road, Jesse at her side. The old wolf stood watching. The pup had sunk back into the trees the minute Jesse arrived.

She shined her flashlight on the boots, black sweater, skinny jeans and a man's black leather jacket.

He lifted the clothes and studied them for a long time.

"Well?" She shifted impatiently.

"The jacket belongs to my cousin. He left it at the cabin one night. The jeans and sweater are Layla's."

"I don't get it. What does this mean?"

"It means we're going hunting."

"What?"

"I brought two backpacks." He strode to the SUV,

threw open the door, pulled out two backpacks and a rifle.

Before she could answer, he turned to the old wolf. "You're the only one that's going to be able to find them."

"Why are you talking to that wolf?" As if she hadn't been talking to him earlier.

The wolf growled low in its throat then crossed the road. The young pup barked then started to follow, staying as far from the humans as possible. The old wolf turned, snapping and snarling. The message clear. Stay. The pup slunk back across the road and into the underbrush where it howled. A heartbreaking, lonely sound.

The hair on the back of her neck rose. Her spidey sense crawling in a hole and hiding.

Jesse tossed her a backpack and headed into the woods.

She drew on the backpack and trotted after him, as both he and the wolf were swallowed up by the dark.

"How do you know we aren't just following this guy on a wild goose chase?" she huffed out after the second mile of jogging in inky black, flashing her light in front of her. She was in good shape. Her blood had built back up, she could do two miles with no problem. But to jog indefinitely?

Jesse didn't reply, just continued trotting after the wolf, his shadow long and fluid in the night, along with the bare limbed trees that swayed and crackled in the wind. The noise and shadows adding an eeriness to Blair's already jumpy nerves.

Another mile passed before Blair tried again. "We seem to be heading toward the rez."

Again. No response.

They hiked several more miles. The wolf had pulled ahead. Now they followed him by the sound of his sporadic howls. Blair's tendons were starting to ache, along with her lungs. She stiffened her spine. If Jesse could do this so could she. She tripped on a rock and saw the ground rising up to meet her when he caught her.

"Are you alright?"

"Fine," she gasped over her thundering heart.

The moon fought free of a shadowy cloud. It trailed and shined full on his face as he eyed her up and down then reached in his pocket and pulled out his phone. "Timothy, I need you to pick me and Chief Deputy Delaney up at the base of the dirt road that leads to my cabin. That's right. Now." He shut down the phone and stuck it in his pocket.

"You can go back if you want but I'm going on. Mateo may be in trouble." She forced her tight, aching muscles to straighten.

"He certainly inspires loyalty in his crew." His voice even, his face expressionless as he spoke.

"Come on, Jesse. You know he'd do the same for us or you."

"For you perhaps. He's abandoned me before."

"What happened?" She'd never understood the divide between these two men.

"You'd have to ask him."

"You've said that before."

"Nothing's changed since the last time I said it."

"Fine." She readjusted her backpack. "See you later."

He laid a detaining hand on her shoulder. She narrowed her eyes. "You don't want to do that."

"You're as prickly as a cactus." He heaved a long sigh. "We're going to the cabin and we'll get there a lot quicker if we drive."

Her jaw went slack. "Why?"

"Because I think that's the vicinity we'll find them in. Now we better get going, it's another two miles to the road."

"Alright." Bewildered, she agreed. She had no better ideas and her feet and legs were killing her.

In another mile they crossed onto the rez. Rather, Jesse crossed. She hobbled. They continued forward, the land sloping upward. By the time they reached the patrol car, it was all she could do to keep from throwing herself on the patrol officer and weeping.

She crawled in the back as Jesse got in the front.

"Drive to my cabin."

The road wound upward. Ten miles and fifteen minutes later the cruiser pulled in front of a small wooden cabin.

The few minutes off her feet had given her a boost. She hopped out of the car.

"What do you want me to do, Chief?" Timothy asked.

Jesse who'd also gotten out of the car leaned on the open passenger window. "Pick up George. Have him drop my SUV here. Follow him and give him a lift back."

"Where is it?"

"Off the road on Mateo's property line on the north side."

"Will do."

Timothy backed up the cruiser, turned around and headed back, his headlights shining through the trees. The hair on her arms rose as glittering gold eyes looked back from the limb of a bare-branched, wide-trunked tree. A huge owl flapped its long wings and flew off.

She shook herself and turned to Jesse. "Now what?"

"We listen for the old wolf."

"Should we go in and look around?"

He shrugged. "If it would make you feel better."

"You don't think they're here."

"The property feels deserted. Plus, the old wolf would be nearby."

"I'd feel better checking it out."

"Knock yourself out. It's not locked."

She sighed. "Of course not." She strode to the cabin, let herself in and walked around flashing her light. It was small, nothing more than a hunting cabin, with one bedroom, a main room, a bathroom and small kitchen. It was surprisingly neat.

In the bedroom, an old five by seven on a pine dresser caught her eye. She picked it up. Two boys laughed into the camera, unmistakably Jesse and Mateo. If Mateo had indeed turned his back on his friend, it had cut Jesse deeply. She set the picture down. Could she trust Jesse or did he have an ulterior motive?

Deep in thought she stepped back outside, just in time to hear a wolf howl. Then another and another all coming from different directions.

CHAPTER 22

"Well hell."

She tromped up to Jesse who stood listening in the moonlight.

"Which one is ours?"

He held a finger to his lips.

The echoes from the howls rolled through the mountains then finally quieted.

She started to speak. He shushed her again.

Once again, a howl came from higher up the mountain, picked up by wolves on a lower terrain.

"We follow that one. The others are just joining in. Here. While I waited, I cut off a couple of branches to use as walking sticks."

"Great. I thank you and my feet and legs thank you."

The sticks helped them make better time, offering support, taking their weight.

As they climbed, it became evident they were getting closer. The old wolf's cries were stronger. The lonely howls from the other wolves faded.

Diamond-bright stars shone from a charcoal sky while a full moon flirted with misty, gauzy clouds.

They stepped onto the ledge. The old wolf paced

back and forth at the edge of the drop.

Her heart in her throat, Blair rushed to the end of the rocky shelf. It began to crumble. She swayed wildly. Jesse reached out and yanked her back.

"Thank you." Her heart pounded a vicious rat-a-tat-tat in her chest.

With a shaky hand, she flashed the light downward. Afraid to look. Afraid of what she'd see. Jesse tensed beside her.

"Is it—" Her voice quavered.

He didn't respond.

She glanced at him. His features rigid, his expression strained. She forced herself to look down. Her breath went out in a whoosh of relief. "It's two dead wolves."

Jesse didn't respond. He pulled off his backpack and yanked out a rope, tied it to the nearest tree and shimmied down the precipice.

"What are you doing? We've got to find Mateo." Mateo. Mateo. Mateo echoed in the night.

Between the flashlight and the moon, she could see Jesse bent over the wolves.

"The male is alive, barely. The female is gone. Go to the house and grab a couple of blankets from the chest at the foot of my bed." His voice, devoid of emotion, carried up the ravine, still she had to strain to hear.

"We don't have time for this. We have to find Mateo. Just shoot it. It'd be kindest in the long run." It was all she could do not to ring her hands. What the hell was wrong with Jesse?

The old wolf turned on her, showing fangs.

224

"Whoa."

It stalked her, eyes fixed and menacing.

She backed up slowly, reaching for her gun.

"This wolf is stalking me," she called. Though what the hell Jesse could do about it from there, she had no idea.

"Just go, Blair. He won't hurt you."

"Yeah, easy for you to say," she muttered under breath. She took another step backward. The wolf took another step forward. It no longer snarled. Alert, it watched her. She took another step back toward the trail. He followed. Her head pounded in time with her heart. She didn't know what was going on, but it was weirding her out. There were forces at work she didn't understand. And she was losing precious time arguing. Her shoulder blades quivering, she turned and trotted down the trail toward the cabin, her hand still on the gun. If it even acted like it was going to attack her, she'd shoot it.

She glanced over her shoulder. The wolf kept its distance, pacing himself behind her.

Fifteen minutes later she arrived at Jesse's. Out of breath, she rushed into the cabin. In the bedroom, she opened a rough-hewn chest with leather straps and dragged out two sturdy blankets. Both beautifully made with bright streaks of color. One aqua and black. One red and yellow.

She bulleted back up the trail, determined to do this and get back to tracking Mateo. By this time, she feared the worst. The thought that he might be dead had her moving even faster, pumping her arms for better momentum. Halfway there she realized the wolf was no longer with her. Hadn't been since she'd arrived at the cabin.

Wheezing, she sped to the ledge. "Here ya go." She tossed the two blankets over as the moon tried to break through a mist that had settled over the horizon. Muted light behind a hazy curtain. She stepped cautiously to the edge and leaned over. She squinted trying to see through the haze. She could now make out the wolves. Their forms wavery and blurred. She put a hand over her eyes and stared harder. The larger one had fallen on top the smaller. It was hard to tell but the smaller one reminded her of the one that had tracked her to her cabin. Was it the wolf that had attacked her and Opel and Rose?

She squatted down for a better view.

Grunting, Jesse bundled the larger wolf into one of the blankets. He knotted the fabric, running the end of the rope through the knots of the rough material.

For a long moment, he stared at the small black wolf then ran a hand over it in a caress before dropping the other blanket over it.

"I need you to haul him up." He pushed to his feet.

Great. She didn't doubt the damn thing weighed as much as she did.

"I've got it." The words came from behind her.

For the second time, she nearly took a header down the side of the ravine.

"Mateo." At the familiar voice, joy surged through her. She shone the light in his face as she whipped around, ready to fling her arms around him. Protocol be damned.

Every bit of blood in her body pooled at her feet.

It wasn't Mateo, but it could be in another twenty or thirty years. The same startling amber eyes, the same thick thatch of hair only silver instead of silver streaked. It fell past his ears. A firm jaw, ears flat against his head and a well-toned body, beneath a shirt that strained across the chest and worn jeans a good two inches too short for him. She frowned. She could have sworn she'd seen that shirt on Jesse. And... he was barefoot.

"Who are you?" Her voice came out ruder than she'd intended, but she'd had all the shocks her system could handle.

He ignored her question and leaned over the edge. "Are you ready?"

Jesse showed no surprise whatsoever at the mysterious stranger who'd materialized in the mist. "He's secure."

Muscles in a lean body rippled as the stranger began hauling him up. Blair got behind him and pulled too. The blanket bumped and bounced against the edge of the sandstone cliff. Close to the top, it snagged on a bush.

The stranger leaned forward. It was just out of reach. He got on his belly and crawled along the edge. Still he couldn't reach him.

Blair's impatience mounted, churning inside her, making her edgy. If they were going to find Mateo, it looked like they'd have to deal with the damn wolf first.

She shoved the older man out of the way and got on her belly. "Hold my feet."

Out of Mateo's eyes, he studied her then gave an abrupt nod and grabbed her ankle. She leaned down as far as she could, her fingers stretched out. "Give me a few more inches." Her voice breathless from the air being pushed out of her belly. She reached again. The blanket brushed her fingertips. "A little farther."

"You can't go any further," the stranger called.

"Just a damn inch. Surely, you can do that."

She squirmed forward. For a moment, she felt his grip loosen. Her life flashed in front of her eyes. The good. The bad. And Mateo. She had to save him.

The grip on her boots tightened and her breathing evened. She got a firm hold on the blanket and pried it from the bush that tangled it. The wolf stared at her from Mateo's eyes. She was seeing him everywhere.

"Haul me up. I've got him."

Her body bumped along the rough crevices for what felt like an eternity but in actuality was only seconds. The man pulled her to her feet with one hand, the other on the rope. Together they hauled up the wolf.

"Let's get Jesse up." She didn't glance at the wolf. Just concentrated on helping Jesse who was climbing the crevice.

When he reached the top, the old man pulled him into his arms. "Forgive me. It was my fault Mateo quit speaking to you. I ordered him to. He lost a true and faithful friend. It's all my fault."

"He could have said no." Jesse stood without

moving, his face expressionless except for pain that lurked in his eyes.

What the hell was going on? Was this man Mateo's father? And if so where had he come from? She thought he'd retired to Puerto Rico. She decided it was time to end a hurtful nonproductive exchange. Why weren't they focusing on Mateo? "Okay the wolf is up. Can we go find Mateo now?"

Two pair of piercing eyes turned to her.

In two, long-legged strides the older man reached the wolf and squatted down.

When he pulled back the blanket, Blair bit back a gasp. So much blood. Why had they bothered? The animal couldn't possibly survive. It would be much kinder to put it out of its misery.

"I'm going to get you home then take care of you." The man she took to be Mateo's father gave the animal a gentle pat then drew back a bloody hand.

"If you two aren't going to end this I am. That poor creature is suffering."

She pulled her Glock, her vision blurred with unshed tears. Righteous determination straightened her spine.

"I can't let you do that, my dear." The older man stepped in front of her.

Jesse swung around and gave her an inscrutable look. "Not that I haven't thought about it, but I don't think that's a good idea."

"He's suffering."

Jesse actually laughed. He spoke to the wolf. "So, what are your thoughts on Blair putting you out of your misery? I bet she's thought about it before too."

The wolf lifted its lip in a poor attempt at a snarl.

Her brain whirled. What the hell? Move over Alice, I'm tumbling down the rabbit hole, again.

"You're going to have to show her sooner or later. Looks to me to be sooner."

"What are you talking about?" Her gaze whipped toward Jesse who stood there grinning. "There's nothing remotely funny about this."

"Well, yeah there is. He'll never forgive you if you shoot him."

"We don't have time for this," the older man said tersely.

Her gaze shot back to the wolf. Never moving a muscle the wolf held her gaze. She could have sworn it sighed. Then for one brief moment the wolf was gone and Mateo lay bleeding on the ground. Then as if unable to hold human form the wolf was back.

For the first and last time in her life, she fainted.

~*~

Muffled voices sounded above her.

"Come on, Blair. Wake up."

Jesse? She shut her eyes tighter. Something too strange to comprehend waited for her once she regained consciousness.

"Just pick up the girl. I'll take Mateo."

"She's the Chief Deputy, Mr. Grey." Jesse scooped her up.

"I know who she is."

"You don't approve."

"I don't approve of her knowing what my son is."

Oh God. There it was. Mateo.

"She won't say anything."

"She better not." The voice growled. Really growled.

She shivered and pried open her eyes. "Put me down, Jesse."

He lowered her to the ground. "We've got to keep moving."

She fell in step with him as Mr. Grey carrying the wolf—carrying Mateo—fell into step behind them.

"Was the SUV at the cabin when you got there?" Jesse asked pushing a tree limb out of the way and holding it till Mr. Grey got through.

"No."

"Want me to carry him?"

"I've got him." Mr. Grey's voice strained. "We're stronger than mere humans and this blanket has helped stop the bleeding. Still I'm sure he's in a great deal of pain."

She fell silent trying to absorb the fact that Mateo was a shapeshifter. That shapeshifters were real. She'd known there was something different about him since the first moment she'd met him, but she'd never seen this coming. No siree.

The going was surprisingly quick considering Mateo's dad carried a full-grown wolf. Pebbles rolled and branches crackled as they hurried down the trail. Jesse pulled out his phone and dialed. "Tim, are you there yet?"

"You had a flat, Chief. Had to change it. We're on

our way."

Jesse shoved the phone in his pocket. "The cruiser's not here yet. You can take him to the cabin."

Mr. Grey nodded.

Five minutes later they hit the clearing and headed inside.

Jesse tossed the throw on the back of a worn cream-colored couch on the cushions. "Lay him down here." He looked at Mateo. "Don't pee on the couch."

The wolf peeled his lips back in a weak snarl.

"Mateo, you're going to have to shift. I need to see what's wrong," his father said.

The wolf closed his eyes and shifted into human form.

Blair bit back a gasp. The man one mass of bruises, his body black, blue and bloody. Before she could think, she said, "Shouldn't he be in a hospital. He may have internal bleeding."

Everyone stared at her, including Mateo.

Jesse snorted "Get it together, Blair. You know, we can't do that."

"I know. I know. For a moment I forgot." She actually rung her hands. Then to her intense surprise Mateo held out his. She took it and her topsy-turvy world righted.

"My dad was a medic in the army. He can take care of me."

The man gave her a brief nod.

"Dad, this is Chief Deputy Blair Delaney. Delaney, my dad. Leonard Grey."

"Sir."

"Young lady." He nodded his head then turned his attention back to his son.

"I won't say anything."

"I beg your pardon?" Mr. Grey's head swiveled back in her direction.

"I heard you as I was coming to. I won't say anything."

"I'll hold you to that." His attention returned to Mateo. "Where does it hurt?"

"Everywhere. I think a few of my ribs are either cracked or broken and Delilah managed to slash my shoulder fairly deep with her knife."

"Jesse, get me some water, clothes, a needle and thread, and some bandage wraps."

Jesse nodded and stole away.

"Thank you for coming out of your self-imposed seclusion to save me."

"You're my son. Nothing is more important to me than you." His voice mild and rusty from lack of use. His gold eyes nearly orange with worry and pain. That he loved his son there could be no doubt.

"What can I do?" Tension built and tightened between her shoulders. Wolf and sickness overlaid Mateo's usual woodsy scent. His eyes sunken and ringed. A large dark bruise stood out on his cheek. Scratches scarred his face. One ran from his nose to his ear.

His stillness bothered her most of all. Mateo was such a vibrant soul, pulsating with life. She reached over and gently pushed back the black and silver hair that had fallen over his forehead.

His eyes opened. "So, you were going to shoot me and put me out of my misery."

The comment relieved her. There was the old Mateo.

"Seemed like a good idea at the time."

Jesse glided in and sat a tray on a honey-colored pine table near the couch. It held a basin of water. A wash cloth and towel. Gauze wrap bandages. Needle and thread. Hemp oil and a styptic stick.

Mr. Grey gave a short nod of approval. He held Mateo's head and gave him a couple of drops of hemp for the pain. Then he began to swab away the dirt and the blood. The blanket hovering at his chest slipped to the floor and Blair caught sight of six pack abs that were unfortunately black and blue, a tight belly and long muscled legs that were covered with fine black hair. She forced herself not to stare at his manhood especially with Mateo's gaze locked on hers.

She recovered, wiggled her eyebrows and winked at him. To her surprise, he turned a dull red.

"Young lady, if you still want to help, hold him upright so I can wrap his ribs."

"I can sit up myself."

But he offered no resistance when she swung his feet to the floor then walked to the back of the couch and held him in place while his dad rolled the wide ace bandage tightly around him.

Mateo grunted and closed his eyes. For one moment, he shimmered and his outline became hazy, the wolf visible. He pushed his fists against the sagging cream-colored couch and came back.

Blair's head spun in a dizzying swirl. She pinched herself then yelled.

Jesse, who'd been watching her, grinned.

She gave him a sickly grimace.

When Mr. Grey finished with the bandage, he pulled out the needle and thread. "Here take a few more drops." He gave him more hemp then began to sew.

Trying to distract herself from the needle biting in then pulling through flesh, she cleared her throat and asked, "How long have you known, Jesse? Obviously longer than I."

"Good question." Mateo gritted his teeth as the thread pulled through his skin then looked at Jesse.

"Since the last time we camped out. You shifted in your sleep. Scared the bejesus out of me." He gave a lopsided grin.

Mateo's eyes widened and his jaw dropped. "Why didn't you say something?"

"Why didn't you?"

"Touche."

"I told you, Jesse, I wouldn't let him. If you need to blame someone, blame me." Mr. Grey continued to sew.

"He should have known better." Jesse cocked his chin at a stubborn angle. Hurt flared briefly in his eyes.

"You're right. Regardless of what Pop said, I should have told you. I was young, scared and stupid."

Jesse blinked at the admission then got his face back to its normally impassive state.

"How old were you?" Blair leaned forward, caught up in the story.

"Thirteen."

"So, it was sort of like having a wet dream."

Three pair of male eyes drilled her.

"In a manner of speaking," Mateo responded dryly.

Someone knocked briskly at the door.

"That's probably Tim." Jesse strode out on the porch. Before he shut the door, a brisk cool breeze blew in, carrying the opened bandage wrap to the floor.

Mateo turned toward her, slow and stiff, and took her hand. She clasped it and again everything in her settled, the impossible, the unbelievable, the woo-woo.

"So, what is your spidey sense telling you now?" he asked.

"It's fried all circuits."

He gave a low chuckle then winced and grabbed his ribs.

Jesse stepped back in, jangling car keys just as Mr. Grey finished knotting the thread and clipped it. "You need a good night's sleep. You may not be one hundred percent when you wake up, but I guarantee you'll be seventy-five."

"The cruiser's out front. Let's go."

"I wouldn't say no if you offered to loan me a pair of pants, preferably those soft buckskins you like so much."

With long easy strides, Jesse disappeared into the bedroom and came back with a flannel shirt and some buckskin pants.

"Young lady, would you dispose of this for me?" Mr. Grey thrust the tray containing bloody water, bandages and instruments at her.

Blair dumped the bloody water in the toilet and the used bandages in the trash. Jesse would have to deal with the rest. Parched, she pit stopped in the kitchen for a glass of water. The same dream catcher as Mateo's hung over the sink. Her heart hurt for the years of lost friendship. She had a feeling now the door had opened it wouldn't close again.

She glugged down the water and headed back to the living room. Mateo had pulled on pants and his dad was helping him into a red and black plaid, flannel shirt. The pants were too short as was the shirt, but it would definitely do.

Jesse stood waiting by the door. As soon as she walked in, he said, "Let's go."

She and Mr. Grey pulled Mateo up and between them walked him to the cruiser. Yellow light from an ancient porch lamp lit the ground in front of them.

Jesse opened the back door and Mateo dropped in, his head flopping back against the seat.

Mr. Grey got in the front and Blair got in the back with Mateo, balling up an empty candy wrapper. She grinned. So, the chief had a sweet tooth. Who'd a thought?

Everyone settled in, Jesse headed the cruiser down the mountain, his passengers bouncing in place whenever he hit a rut.

"She was dead?" Mateo's eyes met Jesse's in the rearview mirror.

"Yes."

"For your sake, I'm sorry."

"You could have warned me, you know."

"Years ago I could have." His voice held a sad quality, she'd never heard before.

"And who's fault is that?"

Blair sighed. Mr. Grey snapped. "The fault is mine. You two are just going to have to work past it."

A grin tugged at her lips. It was probably the same tone he'd used to the boys years ago.

Everyone lapsed into silence. Mateo began to nod. As he slid in the seat, she laid his head in her lap. The cruiser's lights lit up stark black trees whose branches waved like skeletal fingers in the night.

She longed to run her fingers through his hair but knew there would be none of the usual springiness and crispness that usually gleamed from it. Instead she rubbed the pressure between her eyes that had never left since this crazy night began.

Mateo had always seemed unassailable, a bad ass. Now he was sick and instead of a bad ass, she discovered he was a big bad wolf. And wondered for the hundredth time if she was just having a crazy dream and would wake up. When Jesse hit a bump that had her bouncing off the ceiling and rubbing her head, she had serious doubts about the dream.

Finally, they pulled into Mateo's place, where the pup sat waiting on the porch, his tongue hanging out. They helped Mateo out of the car. Blair's shoulder under his left arm and his dad's under his right. Instead of racing away like he usually did, the pup came racing up to them yipping. He skidded to a stop in front of Mr. Grey, clearly confused. Wagging his tail one moment, barking the next and running a few yards away.

The muted glow from the porch light glistened on the silver hairs of Mateo's bowed head. His bare feet made no sound on the wooden planks as they crossed into the house.

His dad lay him on the bed and threw a brilliant-colored star quilt over him. Mateo murmured something unintelligible then fell back asleep. Mr. Grey looked at his son for a long moment then turned his attention to Blair. "Are you staying with him?"

"Yes." She nodded.

"If you need me, I'm around."

She nodded again. He walked out of the room and murmured a few words to Jesse then the outer door clicked shut.

Jesse strode in. "I called Rose and told her Mateo nor you would be in tomorrow."

"What excuse did you give?"

"He's got food poisoning. You're taking care of him."

She snorted. "Mateo has a cast iron stomach."

He shrugged. "Call me if you need me."

"Thanks, Jesse."

Before he reached the door, she called, "Jesse."

He turned. "Yes?"

"Why does Mateo's dad stay in wolf form and never leave the property? Up until tonight, anyway."

"He saw some horrors as a medic. Then about the

time Mateo got out of the Marines, there was a car accident. A little girl was killed. Wasn't Mr. Grey's fault, but that's the last time I saw him. After that a gray wolf started hanging out on the property."

He saluted her and left.

The quiet of the cabin enclosed her. She walked to the window. The moon full and large shone down on the old wolf and the pup on the outskirts of the pines. The old wolf looked directly at her. She raised a hand then walked back to the bed.

Tired beyond belief, she crawled on top of the covers of Mateo's king size bed and fell fathoms deep into slumber.

The sun peeping through the east window woke her, bathing the pine walls and turning them gold. A sharp breeze blew in the window that was cracked an inch. She burrowed into the plain navy duvet that she'd crawled under at some point during the night, rolled over and stared into glittering amber eyes.

"Never expected to find you in my bed, Delaney. Fanaticized a lot about it, but never expected it."

She cleared her suddenly dry throat. "I need a drink," she croaked and hopped out of bed, sprinted to the bathroom where she relieved herself, found some toothpaste and brushed her teeth with her finger. She drank about a gallon of water then took a glass back to Mateo.

"How are you feeling?" She handed him the glass. He was leaning against the bed board and looked more rumpled and sexy than a sick man had a right to. Maybe it was a wolf thing. For the life of her, she

240

couldn't figure out why she wasn't freaking out about that. Maybe at some level she'd always known. There was too much animality in Mateo for him not to be animal.

He patted the bed. "Aren't you coming back?"

"I don't think so." She took a wary step back.

"You should humor me. I'm sick you know."

"You don't look sick." Even the scratch that ran from his nose to his ear had disappeared.

"I'm feeling much better, but I could take a turn any minute. Have you called Luke?"

Luke! She hadn't even thought of him. Hadn't talked to him since she'd talked him out of accepting the job in Billings.

"I better do that now."

"When you do, tell him there will be no more phone sex."

"Now why would I tell him that?" Her eyebrows shot up.

"Because you're in a relationship. A closer one." With a swift move, he yanked her down on top of him and only winced a little when she landed on his ribs. One hand on her waist, he drew her head down.

She yanked it back up. "If you think I'm going to be another notch on your belt, Grey, you're sadly mistaken."

He loosened his hold. With delicate fingers, the hand behind her head came around and pushed a stray strand of hair behind her ear. "Delaney, I fell for you when you first came swaggering through my door, with the voice of an angel and the mouth of a trucker. Which by the way, I'd like to see if it works as well as my fantasies of it."

She stared at him in disbelief, her heart pounding hard.

"Come on, Delaney. Your biological clock is ticking. Don't you think it's time you settled down, got married?"

The voice teased, but intensity shone from his eyes and worry rode his rugged features.

"You want to get married?" Her head spun. Her pounding heart jumped, swelled then settled. She made a token protest. "Your dad doesn't like me."

"Give him some grandkids to play with and he'll be putty in your hands."

"Little wolf boys and girls?"

He stilled. "Not necessarily. Maybe." He shrugged. "Does that bother you?"

"I don't know. Having children with a shifter—the whole shifting thing is unchartered territory."

"Would marrying a shifter bother you?" His body stiffened and his voice cooled.

Whatever he was, he was who she belonged with. Who she wanted. Her heart had known it all along even if her head had failed to acknowledge it.

"Not one damn bit." And jumped him. Her mouth hungry, she pressed herself against him. Her hands only gentling when she touched his shoulder or the bandage holding his ribs in place. He grinned and flipped her over, taking control, his hands everywhere, stripping her clothes till there was nothing between them but his bandage. He caught her hands, looked at her hungrily then took her. She wrapped her legs around him and rose up to meet him. Moments later they exploded together.

"Definitely better than phone sex," she gasped out.

CHAPTER 23

"Good to know." Ignoring the twinges to his slashed shoulder and his bandaged ribs, he decided the pleasure far outweighed the pain.

"You were serious about marrying me, right? It wasn't just a heat of the moment reaction?" He asked the question as casually as possible. Not wanting her to know how much it mattered. He hadn't been joking when he said he'd wanted her since he'd first seen her. The attraction had hit him fast and hard. He'd tried to tell himself it was just lust. But he'd only been kidding himself. Now that she knew the truth about him there was nothing standing in his way, except possibly her feelings.

"You mean like an 'Oh, baby, I love you' that guys are always laying on some susceptible female to get them in the sack?"

A loud pounding on the door had Blair jumping for her clothes. Before she could get them on, he grabbed her hand. "Were you serious?"

"Of course I was, you fool." She kissed him hard on the mouth with her wet, ripe mouth. "I love you enough, I'll even have your puppies."

"Babies. You'd have babies." He ground out,

irritated. "Regardless, there's no guarantees they'd be shifters." Then he caught the gleam in her eye.

"Very funny." He grumbled.

"I thought so." She laughed and began throwing on her clothes.

Again, he reached for her hand.

"I've got to get dressed." She tugged at it.

Still holding on, he drew open the door of his pine night stand and pulled out a worn, gray velvet ring box. He flipped open the lid and slid a plain oval turquoise, edged with silver, on her finger. "It was my mom's."

A radiant smile lit her face and she held it out to admire. "I love it."

"Boss. Blair. Are you here?"

"Oh my God, it's Rose." Blair's face turned ashen. She hopped into her pants and tossed on her shirt, not bothering with underwear. "Why can't people lock doors around here?"

Mateo chuckled as she buttoned her shirt crooked. "I'll be out in a minute."

Blair slipped out the door. "I'm coming, Rose."

Mateo pulled on his jeans and carefully shoved his arms through a gray cabled fisherman's sweater. He padded into the living room and stopped in surprise in the doorway. Quinn was with Rose, his arm around her. Both had Montana-wide smiles on their faces and a good-sized diamond gleamed on Rose's left hand.

Rose saw him first. "How are you, Boss?"

"I couldn't possibly be any better. Congratulations."

"We wanted you two to be the first to know."

Mateo took two long strides to Quinn's side, gave him a hearty handshake then kissed Rose's cheek. They were an unusual match but no more so than he and Blair. Puppies, indeed. He grinned to himself.

"So, when's the wedding?" He asked, as Blair nudged him out of the way to admire Rose's ring.

"I don't know. We only got engaged this morning. Quinn asked me over breakfast." Her face turned beet red at what she'd revealed.

"No longer sleeping on the couch, Quinn?" Blair teased as Mateo said, "Isn't that a coincidence."

Rose gave him a confused look. He put his hands in his pockets, rocked on his heels and smiled back. She glanced at Blair's left hand and her eyebrows rose in a questioning expression.

"It was Mateo's mom's." And now it was Blair wearing the Montana-wide smile.

"Oh, honey, that's wonderful." Rose reached out and hugged first Blair then Mateo while Quinn just looked on in confusion.

Rose explained. "They're engaged too, Quinn dear."

His jaw dropped and his eyebrows rose to his hairline before he grabbed Blair in a bear hug then pumped Mateo's hand so vigorously Mateo winced.

"I don't suppose you've got any champagne around here so I can make some mimosas to toast with, do you?" Blair asked.

"Actually, I think there may be a bottle left from last New Year." A dark stubble of chin whiskers rasped as he rubbed them.

They all trooped into the kitchen. He rummaged in the back of the pantry till he found the champagne, drew it out and blew the dust off of it. Blair took it, found the orange juice and made mimosas, placing the drinks in plain glasses since Mateo's dishware didn't run to crystal. After they toasted, Rose decided to fix them all breakfast. As the bacon sizzled and she scrambled eggs, Mateo cleared his throat. "You no longer have to worry about any more attacks, Rose."

"You caught the perp?" Quinn asked in the process of raising a stone mug filled with steamy fragrant coffee to his lips.

"I thought you had food poisoning. Though, I guess you wouldn't want breakfast if that was the case." Rose looked understandably confused. Quinn shrugged. Blair just waited, curious to see what spin he was going to put on this.

Mateo took out sturdy earthenware plates from the cabinet. Blair took her cue and got out the silverware, her ears all but twitching.

"I think Jesse figured I'd want to give you the detes."

"Well?" Quinn leaned forward.

"Blair was right." He glanced at his fiancée as he set the plates on the counter beside the stove. Rose began to fill them. "Only it was a woman and her wolfdog."

"What happened?" Rose popped bread into the toaster.

We chased them to the rez. By that time Jesse had

joined us. We tracked them into the mountains. It had grown dark. The woman lost her footing and they both went over a cliff."

"Who was it? Did you recover the body?" Quinn's stomach growled loudly.

Rose filled a plate with bacon, eggs and toast.

Mateo set it in front of Quinn.

"No, I didn't. It's a tribal matter now. Jesse made it clear I was to butt out, he'd handle it. And if there's one thing that can be said for Jesse Kipp, where the law is concerned, he doesn't bend. As far as I'm concerned, the case is closed. The woman and wolf are dead. No one could have survived that fall. We may never know who the woman was."

Blair grabbed the next plate that Rose filled and sat down. She'd have to call Jesse and fill him in. Her daddy had always told her not to lie unless you have to and when you do put as much truth in it as possible. Well there was a lot of truth to Mateo's story if you overlooked no one would be able to survive and to be fair he wouldn't have survived if he hadn't landed on top. And considering the aliases the woman used he didn't really know who she was. Yup, couldn't get closer to the truth than that. She bit into her toast and chewed.

Rose finished filling the plates and she and Mateo sat down. She looked at Mateo and grinned wide enough to show her molars. "You know what this means don't you, Boss?"

"What?"

"We're going to win the election."

~*~

A week later, beaming from ear to ear, Adam came running in brandishing a newspaper. He thumped one on each desk. The headline read:
SHERIFF GREY BEATS ETHERIDGE.
By Jeremy Haskins

EPILOGUE

Such a strange week.

With the sharp scent of wild mint in his nostrils, Jesse walked up the mountain path, a shovel strapped to his back and a rope wrapped around his shoulder. This was the first opportunity he'd had to come back. The sun shone on his face, warming him one minute, the next it raced behind hulking gray cumulus clouds. In the distance thunder rumbled. Again, the sun peeked out. Again, it hid.

It must surely be female with its propensity to be coy, he mused. Reaching overhead, he plucked a pinecone from a nearby tree then lobbed it into space. Blair being the exception. She was the most straightforward female he had ever met, more like an eagle than a sun. Mateo was lucky. They would complement each other, as he once thought he and Layla did. How had Layla hidden the perversity in her soul? Or that she was one such as Mateo, only evil?

Still he had cared for her and was determined to honor her remains with a proper burial. Here in the mountains where she'd roamed wild. As cool as the weather was, he doubted the body had started to decompose. He'd placed rocks around the corners of the blanket to keep it in place and the carrion feeders out.

When he reached the ledge, he looked down. The red and black blanket, that slashed across the natural browns and greens of the ledge, still in place. He removed the rope, tied it securely to a nearby pine and lowered himself down.

He strode to the blanket and frowned. The rocks were still in place, but the blanket lay flat against the ground. He nudged it with his foot. Nothing. Reluctantly he lifted the fabric.

There was no body. Not so much as a black hair.

Thunder boomed, making him jump. A blinding spear of lightning struck nearby making the hairs on his neck rise. In the distance he heard a wolf howl.

His heart pounded and he scrambled back up the rope. Reaching the top, he didn't even bother to collect the braided cord, just bulleted down the trail. He stopped once and looked behind him. A black wolf stared at him. His breath fast and shallow, his pulse racing, he watched as it shimmered into a beautiful woman. Into Layla. He stopped breathing as she held his gaze. Another hazy shimmer and the wolf was back. It gave him a canine grin then disappeared into the underbrush.

AUTHOR'S NOTE

Just a few factoids.

Grizzly is a fictious town as is everything and everyone in it.

Browning, MT is headquarters of the Blackfoot Reservation. Wanda's is fictious.

The ponderosa pine is the official state tree of Montana.

Last but not least, if you enjoyed *Mateo's Law* enough to leave a review, thank you so much. A good review is an author's bread, butter and favorite ice cream, all rolled into one. I can guarantee, you'll put a smile on my face when I see it.

AND...If you'd like to sign up for my newsletter, the signup is at my blog: sandracox.blogspot.com. I'd love to have you on the list.

ABOUT SANDRA COX

Sandra is a vegetarian, animal lover and avid gardener. She lives with her husband, their dog and cats in sunny North Carolina.

She has written in several different genres. These days she writes all things Western. She is a category bestselling Amazon author, Eppie finalist and Golden Ankh Award winner.

Sandra can be found at http://www.sandracox.blogspot.com If you'd like to stay abreast of what's going on in her world and learn about any new releases you can sign up for her newsletter while you are there. Her twitter handle is: Sandra_Cox and her Amazon page is https://www.amazon.com/stores/Sandra-Cox/author/B002BM3AKC .